The Future Is Nigh

A treasury of short fiction by
Writers of the Future Contest winning authors.

Second Edition.

Published by GotScifi Group

Life's too short. Live more lives. Read.
www.moreLives4me.com

Copyright © 2018 by GotScifi Group

All works copyright © and all rights reserved by their respective authors.

Support quality literature.
Respect copyright.

ISBN-13: 978-1548563912

"Dreams of the Rocket Man" illustration by Riley Hardwick

"Today I Am Paul" illustration by Anne-Mhairi Simpson, incorporating:
Looking into the light © Darrenw | Dreamstime.com and Senior woman asleep
© Wavebreakmedia Ltd | Dreamstime.com

Cover design & print layout by C. Stuart Hardwick.

Contents

Preface 2

Sparg 6
    Brian Trent

Dreams of the Rocket Man 16
    C. Stuart Hardwick

Möbius 42
    J.W. Alden

Rats Will Run 48
    Marina J. Lostetter

Fuel 78
    Matthew S. Rotundo

Miss Davenport's Ugly Cat 88
    C. L. Holland

Last House, Lost House 100
    William Ledbetter

Softly Into the Morning 114
    L. D. Colter

Squalor and Sympathy 134
    Matt Dovey

Today I Am Paul 166
    Martin L. Shoemaker

Preface

When I first entered the Writers of the Future contest, I was just hoping to get some feedback on my writing. I knew the contest was run by Dave Farland and judged by a who's who of my favorite scifi and fantasy authors. I knew L Ron Hubbard had started it back in 1983, back when I used to stand in B. Dalton Bookseller, allowance in hand, weighing my choices between the contest anthology, a book of the year's Hugo winners, or a couple of issues of Starlog or Antic (the Atari resource). I knew that in the decades since, it had grown into a *big deal*, as big in its own way as the Emmys or the Oscars, and that it was nothing at all to do with me.

I never expected to be wrong about that, to win and be flown to Hollywood, to get a chance to learn from Tim Powers (whose excellent novel *On Stranger Tides* inspired a *Pirates of the Caribbean* movie). I never expected to meet Orson Scott Card and Todd McCaffrey, to eat barbecue with legends Larry Niven and Larry Elmore, to appear on stage with Astronaut Leland Melvin and Starlog founder Kerry O'Quin, or to watch a lunar eclipse with Robert J Sawyer. But all that happened.

I also never expected to be welcomed into a new family, a family as diverse as Hufflepuff and as wondrous as the staff at Hogwarts—a family that confidently, insistently, expected great things. But that happened too, and the thing about a family is, we not only get each other's jokes, we help point each other in the right direction.

During the workshop, Mike Resnick chided me for not having joined my local writer's guild, so I did that as soon as I got home. There I met another new family, and that got me a hug from David Gerrold (author of *Martian Child* and "Trouble with Tribbles") and a chance to edit my first anthology (Tides of Impossibility, Skipjack

Press). Then Kevin J Anderson twisted my arm and dragged me to his Superstars writing workshop, and I met Jim Butcher (Dresden Files) and learned about ebook construction from the immaculately mohawked Quincy J Allen. And I became part of yet another tribe.

And so, in 2017, I find myself editing this, a collection of stories by fellow winners of the most prestigious contest for short scifi and fantasy in all the world. Me—the kid who tried to build a helicopter out of swing set parts and a lawnmower engine—not just appearing alongside, but editing those wizards of the bookstore shelves, the likes of whom I've envied for oh so many years—and who I now call friends.

And man, oh man, is it a privilege. I'm a picky, impatient reader, one of those scoundrels who goes through the bookstore reading opening pages and leaving work after work displaced in some small way that the stocking clerk will have to set right—but not here. These are all stories I not only want to read, they're stories *I wish I had written*. Lab rats on the run? Got 'em. Alien pets? Check. Rocket borne dreams? Serlingesque kismet? Teddy bears with soul? Causality loops? Got it all--all the good stuff that made me read scifi as a kid. All the stuff that made me want to become a writer.

In this small volume, I give you two Writers of the Future Gold Pen Award winners, a Jim Baen Memorial Award finalist, a Tangent Online Recommendation, a Nebula award nominee, and a Washington Science Fiction Association Small Press Award winner. And the rest? Well...they only have so many awards to give out, you know. We wouldn't want to be greedy.

Judy Garland was discovered on the stage of the Wilshire Ebell in Hollywood, the same theater where we all accepted our Writers of the Future awards. Today she's remembered for her role in The Wizard of Oz, and the connection is more than passing. I feel like I've retraced her steps, killed a few witches and met the man behind the curtain—only to find him extending a friendly hand. Beyond, the road branches onward into dizzying heights, but the tribe is here, climbing, struggling, beckoning, and the vistas ahead are endless.

Come, dear reader, let us make this journey together.

C Stuart Hardwick, Editor
June 2017, Galveston Texas.

SPARG

First published in Daily Science Fiction (August 2013)

Brian Trent

Sparg had difficulty making pancakes, but he was trying.

In the empty apartment, he clutched the silver bowl with one tentacle to hold it steady. With another, he attempted the far trickier business of whipping the batter as he'd seen his owners do many, many times. The bowl was bigger than him. The counter was sticky with flour, egg, and ink.

From his cage, he had watched them conduct this peculiar ritual enough times to understand it was how they prepared their food. More elaborate than the brown fish-pellets they gave him. When his food dish was empty, they usually noticed as they shuffled in from the bedroom each morning. If they didn't, Sparg would gently thump his tentacles against the bars until they came over to see what was the bother. Then strange sounds would issue from their red mouths:

"Sparg's food dish is empty. Can you get the bag?"

And Sparg would thump his tentacles merrily, knowing that food was coming and that his owners would likely pet him when they refilled his dish, and he liked that. Sometimes he gently wrapped his tentacles around their hands as they did, and he would squeeze his eyes shut and enjoy their warmth and smell and reassuring touch.

The pancake batter reeked. Atop the kitchen counter, Sparg gave the mixture another few stirs. Then he flung the whisk into the kitchen sink, taking small delight in watching the tool float through the air and clatter into the shiny basin.

His owners never had trouble moving the pancake batter from the counter to the stove. That was because they were tall, magnificent beings, striding from room to room on graceful legs. Sparg gripped the bowl with three tentacles and held it aloft as he crawled down the counter, leaving little sucker prints in the dust.

He was not allowed on the kitchen counter or stove. This was a rule he understood. His owners flew into frightful antics when they saw him there. In the beginning, they react mildly enough: lifting him off the counter and returning him to the floor, petting him and issuing stern words. One day, the deepvoiced owner was drinking coffee at the counter when Sparg crawled up to sit near him. Deepvoice yelled and slapped him off, sending him into a low-gravity spin across the room. Sparg had been shocked by the assault, but then he heard Deepvoice laughing and he realized this must be some sort of game.

He returned to the counter at once, to take part in the amusement. When Deepvoice slapped him off a second time, the blow was more painful.

"What are you doing?" asked the high-voiced owner.

"Stupid thing. This is why we should have gotten a dog."

"Dogs and cats don't adjust to the gravity here. Don't hit it again!"

"It keeps coming back here! I thought they were supposed to be smart!"

"It doesn't understand."

"It will."

Highvoice intercepted Sparg as he was limping towards the counter a third time, and she put him in Littlevoice's bedroom. The pain set in when he was alone. Sparg didn't like being alone. He resolved to never go to the counter again.

He reached the floor successfully, the pancake batter wobbling in his desperate grip. The floor glistened from past spills. Sparg scuttled to the stove and began the challenging ascent. The batter sloshed around in the silver bowl as he pulled himself up, one careful inch at a time. At last, he flopped onto the stovetop, fumbled amid pots and pans, dials and spatulas. Then he paused, trying to remember the rest of morning ritual.

Owners awoke and refilled his food dish. Owners went to the kitchen and made breakfast – usually pancakes. Owners...

Ah!

Sparg drew open a cabinet. It was time to make Littlevoice's school lunch.

Each morning, the smallest member of the human trio would receive a brown paper bag filled with fruit, crackers, a juicebox, and sandwich. Sparg tapped the stovetop anxiously, considering the problem's magnitude.

Crackers were plentiful, and there were still several juiceboxes in the fridge. He had no trouble constructing a sandwich, and rather enjoyed prying the peanut butter can open and spreading its creamy contents onto two slices of bread. The problem was the fruit. It didn't look like fruit anymore. Sparg didn't know what had happened. The bananas and apples and pears had changed into a putrid brown jelly, fuzzy and gray with moss.

More carefully than he had handled the eggs, Sparg eased a sagging, lopsided pear from the bowl and – hardly daring to breathe – he gingerly set it into the bottom of the paper bag. Then, breathing again, he scuttled down the stove and deposited the bag by the apartment door. He hesitated there, thumping all his suckered limbs, trying to think.

"Come on everyone! Breakfast!"

Breakfast! Sparg hopped up and down, recalling the clink and clatter of plates. He moved steadily along the floor, grabbed a smooth table leg, and ascended onto the kitchen table. The plates, glasses, and silverware were exactly as he had set them weeks ago. Still, Sparg squinted carefully at each place-setting. Satisfied, he threw himself to the floor, drifting in the low-gravity and remembering old amusements.

He went to the wallscreen. This too was part of the ritual. Deepvoice was typically the first one to awaken each morning, and after coffee he –

–coffee!

Filter, water, coffee, pot, mug! Sparg worked feverishly, swelling with pride that he had figured out the strange contraption. It had never been visible from his cage, and all he knew of its presence was the unpleasant hissing, popping, and trickling noises it exuded. Once the coffee was bubbling with those familiar sounds, Sparg leapt back into the low gravity and pressed the wallscreen to life.

"–second squadrons attempted to break the blockade. The North American continent has… firing of the defense satellite… in retaliation to the… will seek peaceful resolution if…"

The screen warbled and froze.

Sparg felt small as he sat on the rug before the wall of pixelating images. He didn't understand the bright wheeling colors and disembodied heads. But he cast a hopeful glance towards the front door.

Then he saw the football. His color flushed to a dark cobalt.

Sparg didn't like the football.

He used to fight with it, wrapping his tentacles over its toughened skin and trying to crush it. When that failed, he industriously worked to pry it apart at the laces. He wasn't sure how the animosity had begun. It might have been that it reminded him of himself in a curious way: both the same size and similar color. Or perhaps it was the way Deepvoice would cradle and hold it as he watched the wallscreen. When Sparg was alone, he would often stare at the football through his cage bars and seethe.

He stalked the football now. It was nestled against the couch, unaware of him. Sparg flattened his body into a pancake of his own, approaching in an oblique line of predatory flanking…

Something was wrong.

The air smelled of smoke.

In truth, something had been wrong for a long time. Sparg had known it the moment his three owners rushed into the kitchen one morning, bags in their arms.

"The last of the shuttles takes off in two hours! Now hurry!"

"Daddy! Why are we leaving!"

"I told you! Everyone's leaving! We have to get to the shuttleport while it still has transports!" Deepvoice sounded worried. That never happened, and it made Sparg worry.

Something was very wrong.

"But my toys!"

"Leave the goddam toys. We're only allowed two carry-ons. I'll buy you more toys on Earth."

"What about Sparg?"

A pause. Sparg understood the sound of his name. He thumped the cage bars anxiously.

Deepvoice approached the cage. He peered at Sparg for perhaps half a minute. Then he unlatched the lock.

"He'll have to fend for himself. Let's go."

"We can't leave him!"

"No pets! We have to leave now."

"But he'll die without us!"

"Goddamn it, it's just a stupid animal!" A hesitation. "Leave the bag of food open."

"Will we be coming back, Daddy?"

Another pause, longer and graver than the last. "Yes. It's only a war, and all wars end. We'll be back and then you can be with Sparg again."

And then they were rushing towards the apartment door. Sparg scampered after their heels, but they quickly passed through the doorway into the mysterious corridor beyond, and then the door slammed in his face.

And hadn't opened since.

Something was wrong. Sparg smelled the pancakes burning.

Smoke gushed from the stovetop and slithered over the ceiling with black fingers. Sparg's panic exploded, and he left a trail of ink as he pushed off for the stove. He was halfway into his climb when the alarm went off.

This had happened once before. Highvoice had been cooking and had received a phone call. She was in the other room while the food burned, and then the alarm lights flashed and water poured out of the ceiling.

Sparg had liked the water. Liked the feel of it on his skin. While Highvoice shrieked and waved her arms to dispel the smoke, Sparg had splashed merrily around the kitchen floor.

But now, the water brought no joy. Sparg reached the stovetop, wrenched the pan from the red burner, and wielded the spatula to flip the reeking, charred mess. The sprinklers drenched the kitchen. The lights flashed for a while, and then went dead.

They probably wouldn't like the breakfast. Sparg sat atop the kitchen table with the blackened pancakes in each plate. He barely moved. The smoke had given the apartment a greasy patina and now he waited, glancing dubiously at his only other companion: the football, strapped into the old highchair, with a plate of burnt pancake and a cup of juice.

Then he heard the voices in the corridor.

Sparg shivered in anticipation too great to be constrained. He gave the table one last, hasty inspection. Then he leapt off, spinning, all tentacles extended in joy. He hit the wet floor and slid, scrabbling madly towards the door, and waited.

From the corridor came the muted voice:

"—reason to be concerned. A fire has been reported on your floor but has been contained. Please do not panic. Fire safety personnel have been notified and are en route. There is no reason to be concerned. A fire has been reported on your floor but has been contained. Please do not panic. Fire safety personnel have been notified and are en route…"

And then the door opened in his imagination.

His owners rushed in. Deepvoice and Highvoice and Littlevoice reached down to pet him… But the fantasy faded. The door remained an immovable, vertical slab.

Sparg waited.

When evening fell, he kept vigil as long as he could. At last he curled up against the door. When he awoke, he crept through the house to see if they had returned while he slept, and when he saw the empty rooms he stared for many minutes, trying to understand what he had done wrong.

Slowly, feeling his loneliness harden into renewed determination, he returned to the counter and began again.

Briant Trent

Brian Trent's speculative fiction appears in *Analog Science Fiction & Fact*, *Fantasy & Science Fiction*, *Daily Science Fiction*, *Orson Scott Card's Intergalactic Medicine Show*, *Nature*, *Escape Pod*, *Pseudopod*, *COSMOS*, *Galaxy's Edge*, *Apex*, *Penumbra*, *Crossed Genres*, and numerous year's best anthologies. He lives in New England.

Trent's website is www.briantrent.com.

Sparq

Dreams of the Rocket Man

A Jim Baen Memorial Award Finalist • A Tangent Online Starred Recommendation
First published in Analog Science Fiction & Fact (September 2016)

C. Stuart Hardwick

Most folks called him Mr. Coanda, but to us, growing up, he was just the Rocket Man. Saturdays, my brother Keith and I would ride our bikes through the woods to where the barbed wire marking his land had been absorbed by the bark of a towering oak. A hanging muscadine vine made a platform sturdy enough for many a bouncing adventure, and the boughs of a nearby cottonwood formed the rooms of our imagined space cruiser and later the foundation of a serviceable, if piecemeal, tree-house. From this vantage point, we would often spy as the Rocket Man unwittingly led our space fleet into battle, firing small rockets from a concrete pad that must once have been part of a farm building.

We'd watch him prepare, imagining the evil plans behind his latest assault or the glory to be had in its wake. Then we'd answer his volley with all our imagined wonder weapons, all the more real we thought, for the wafting smell of sulfur, gunpowder, and burnt rubber.

One autumn day, Halloween week when I was thirteen, Daddy turned off the highway a bit early and wound through the trees and up to a dark, cedar house like those where I imagined park rangers might live. The effect was completed by unkempt flowerbeds lined with rocks and animal skulls, and feeders ringed by moldering seed husks. Daddy had paid Mr. Coanda to make or repair some part for our garden tractor, and he walked us around the house, through a gate secured with a loop of steel wire, and out to the unpainted barn where Mr. Coanda was working.

While the two men talked, my brother and I stared into the barn's shadowed recesses, where strange and fancy machines of unimaginable purpose stood sentry over countless dusty and forgotten-looking rocket parts. There were nose cones and tail fins and funnel-shaped nozzles, and even the odd bit of electronic gear. When Mr. Coanda had explained to Daddy whatever needed explaining, he noticed our prying eyes and asked if we were interested in rockets. If it was all right with Daddy, he said, we were welcome to come back on Saturday and he would show us how to make one.

I could hardly think of my schoolwork that week, but when Saturday finally came, all he showed us was how to make pop bottles fly with compressed air and water, and then with vinegar and soda. I was a little disappointed, but the ice had been broken. Keith and I became regular guests, soon building our own rockets from balsa and cardboard and sending them up under Mr. Coanda's guidance. He taught us how to measure a rocket's altitude and trajectory, and how to improve its performance through careful tinkering and even more careful note taking. He even let us launch one of his own big multi-stagers, a yellow-striped giant with homemade motors and an on-board camera.

When the Geminids passed, we helped him mulch his strawberry plants and live-trap marauding rabbits. By the Perseids, we had learned to make our own exploding skyrockets and roast popcorn right on the cob. The sun swept on through the zodiac. Keith's dreams turned from rockets to football and girls, mine from store-bought model kits to experimental designs of my own.

The woods grew lush, then dry and brown, then dappled again with buds. Then, over Easter break, I was helping Mr. Coanda mend a barn door hinge when the phone rang inside his house. It was Daddy. Momma and Keith had been in a wreck and were being flown down to Houston. Daddy said they'd be fine, but he needed to go for a few days and would it be okay if I stayed with Mr. Coanda.

That night, Mr. Coanda made chili, then drove me home to pick up clothes and a toothbrush. He stood in the doorway of our cramped little bedroom and waited while I gathered my things. Keith's wall was decorated with hot cars and women, mine with robots and scifi movie stills. I'd made a shelf over my bed on which I'd placed every rocket I could get hold of, including Mr. Coanda's pop bottles and models. When he saw these, he stood still and quiet like grownups did when they were trying to decide whether to say something.

Finally, he stepped inside and pulled the space ship chain pull that worked the ceiling fan light.

"This looks like my room when I was little," he said. His blue eyes, in that moment, were a young boy's eyes, like lights on Christmas morning. The crags and valleys of his withered cheeks shone all the deeper beneath them.

"I'm not little," I said.

He laughed. "Nothing wrong with being little, son. Less mass to boost into orbit."

I was to stay the week. In the morning, he saw me onto the bus and was waiting when it came back, just like Momma used to do. Monday passed without word, and he let me stay up watching movies. Tuesday night, he was showing me how to slice a tomato without crushing the pulp when the phone rang once again. He answered, then stepped in the back room and shut the door. He talked for a while in hushed tones. A decision was being debated, and when he stepped out, he was dull-eyed and gray, and he told me my momma was dead.

He patted my shoulder and said, "Your pa says he'd have liked you to be there, but she never..."

From what I'd been told and what I hadn't, it wasn't really a surprise, but some things you can never prepare for. Though I didn't break down and cry exactly, I felt a torrent down my cheeks and a melon-sized lump in my throat.

Mr Coanda said, "Are you...? Do you folks go to...?" Then he sighed and put me in a chair and set about finishing our dinner. I watched as he added the tomatoes to a sauce and put the knife and cutting board away. As he wiped up the spillage, he said, "You know Jimmy, I was in a plane crash once."

I raised a questioning brow, but I couldn't speak for the lump.

He nodded. "Brand new twin engine turbofan, cracked a blade climbing out of Spokane. Turns out the pilot misread the instruments and shut down the wrong engine."

Having finished his cleaning and toweled off his hands, he pulled out a chair from the table and straddled it to sit. "Quietest thing you ever heard, being in the air with a hundred and forty-three people, no engines, just the wind whistling by. When I saw a steeple pass above the wingtip, I knew we weren't going to make it."

I didn't know why he was telling me this, but I had to ask, "What happened?"

"We crashed. Me and my wife and my baby boy. And you know what I was thinking, just at the end?" I didn't.

"Who's going to mow the grass?"

I couldn't help it. I laughed. "What?"

"We had this cranky old push mower that Millie could never start. I knew I was going to die, and all I could think was, who will cut the grass, now I'm gone? Only I didn't die. The cabin split right at our feet. I was at the window and the wall must have shielded me some but..."

"I'm sorry."

He waved a dismissive hand. "It was a long time ago. I won't say you ever get over it, but you get used to it eventually. Anyhow, it was a similar thing, a stupid accident. But folks'll come around and say it's the Lord's will, part of his great plan... How that's supposed to be better, I never did know. Maybe it just feels better to them because they don't know what else to say. But I'll tell you what might help, is to remember that everybody dies, but our lives are like flames passed from candle to candle. The light's been burning now for millions of years. Your momma carried it for her little while, and you'll carry it for yours — you and your brother and all those kids she taught and helped point in new directions. And I expect that's what she was thinking, when she knew they were going to crash, that you'd all be here to carry the flame."

That helped.

The next morning, Mr. Coanda took me out to the barn and had me help him move an old refrigerator and pry open a large wooden crate. Inside, all packed in gray foam blocks, were parts for a rocket unlike any I'd ever seen. It had three stages, all gleaming aluminum, and when stacked five feet high on a plywood stand, it had a shape like a rifle bullet projecting from one end of an empty toilet paper roll.

"Wow!" I said, "That's a real monster. What is it?" He chuckled a bit. "Just a candle."

I helped him carry the rocket parts down through the woods to the pasture and a cinderblock workshop near his launchpad. We mixed up a gray, putty-like fuel for the first two stages and pressed clay and black power into a cardboard tube for the third.

Mr. Coanda picked up the first stage with his fingers splayed wide over the fins as he pressed tape to an electric igniter. "So what would you say is special about this rocket?"

The first stage seemed like an ordinary booster, although unusually squat. The third, upper, stage was no different from rockets I had built myself except for the elongated motor and thin-walled metal construction. The second stage, though, was a tube within a tube, a fact more conspicuous now with the propellant core in place.

"The second stage, right?"

"Very good." He tapped the outer lip of the stage. "This is a ram intake. It's not a true ramjet, but a ducted rocket."

He explained how the rocket exhaust would suck in air through the outer tube, compress it, and blow it out at high speed.

"Same idea as a propeller on an airplane," he said. "When you're traveling through the air, why not push against it along the way? Build a rocket that can do that like an airplane, and you've got something."

He set the booster down to free his hands for punctuation. "When I was your age," he said, "I thought I'd wind up on the moon. I thought we'd fly there in sleek spaceliners and vacation on Mars. All our dreams seemed before us and we never thought about the economics behind them. But the reality is, space travel is expensive, and that's mostly due to the boosters — the cost of climbing the gravity well."

He said that in space travel, the cost of a launch is determined by all kinds of things, not just the weight of machinery, fuel, and oxidizer, but also the aerodynamics and trajectory which control how much air resistance and gravity a rocket must fight before it reaches orbit.

"Everything's a trade-off," he said. "The Saturn V carried us to the moon and did it in under a decade, but it consumed fifteen tons of propellant every second, and everything scaled up to match."

"Wasn't the Space Shuttle supposed to be cheaper?"

"Sure, and it was a fine piece of engineering, but..." His eyes glazed over and I could see he was revisiting the past. "The shuttle burned hydrogen, which is bulky as hell. That meant a large external tank to drag through the air and accelerate up to orbital speed. It had airplane parts that are just dead weight on a space ship. Hell, the tires weighed as much as the astronauts. It was meant to be a reusable spaceliner. Instead, it was a space station you had to launch over and over again. When the Russians got hold of the design, they thought it must be a smokescreen for an orbital bomber. It lost sight of the prize, see, dollars per pound to orbit."

I looked at the monster rocket. "So is this the solution?"

"This? No. This is just a clue. It's a working scale model of a clever missile the Russians built back in the 1950's." He had asked me to fit a tiny camera into a window below the nose cone. Now he added a transmitter, battery, and chute.

As we carried the stages out to the pad, he continued. "To really open up space," he said, "will take hybridization of ideas. Maybe high-flying planes to carry the rockets, maybe rail launchers for freight, maybe power beams shot from the ground, hell, I don't know."

"If you don't know, nobody does. We might as well give it up."

"But that's the wrong way to look at it, Jimmy. We got into the air when the Wright brothers broke down the problem: propulsion, lift, control. They weren't the smartest or the richest fellows, but they were the first to break it down and take the pieces in turn. Space is no different. We'll get the cost down by reexamining all the pieces.

"nLook at oxygen, the heaviest part of any conventional booster. There's already oxygen in the air, so some people want to build spaceplanes that linger in the upper atmosphere gobbling it up until they're close to orbital speed. But then there's so much heating and drag see, and you have to fly for so long, the fuel weighs as much as the oxygen saved. Everything's a trade-off. Look at this ducted rocket. Instead of just spitting out tons of propellant every second, it grabs some of the air and claws its way up like a cartoon coyote up a falling length of rope."

I laughed, prompting him to add, "Well that could actually work, you know, if you could only pull the rope fast enough!"

I held the second stage while he fit the third into place. "The trouble is, the duct adds weight. Turn it into a ramjet and you get more thrust, so the weight doesn't hurt quite as much. But then you need a pre-booster to reach supersonic speed before the ramjet can work."

"Another trade-off," I said.

"Now you've got it." He looked from my hands to the rocket, indicating where I should hold on.

I moved accordingly. "So what's the answer?" He twisted the stages between his hands to check for snugness, then ran his eyes up the stack. "We just have to find the right trade-offs."

The launch was anti-climactic, the recovery, an adventure. The video, which we viewed in the house over bowls of popcorn and chili, was hypnotic. The rocket climbed and climbed. As it staged and staged again, the ground slowly warped into a fisheye ball. When the propellant finally ran out, the Earth was just an azure band beneath the inky black of space.

Mr. Coanda let a handful of popcorn fall back into the bowl. "Holy hell," he said, "if that ain't a beautiful sight."

I was similarly entranced. "How high do you figure we went?"

"I don't have to figure. I have data. Ah...63,000 feet."

"Wow! That's almost in space!"

"Not quite. Minimum orbit's eight times higher, and then you have to accelerate to orbital velocity in order to stay there."

I stared at the glowing earthscape. "Still..."

"Still," he said, and popped the top off a Nehi. "You'll get there one of these days."

"You think?"

"Sure you will. You'll see."

Keith came home in a wheelchair and spent two years relearning how to walk. I spent that time with Mr. Coanda, learning how to fly. He taught me Tsiolkovsky's equations and the principles of rocketry, from the V2 to the shuttle. He showed me how engines work, how their parts are cooled and lubricated, and how waste energy from one step is often reused to drive another, and he explained how different engines meet different needs. Ramjets are simpler than turbojets but only work in a narrow range of speeds. Scramjets are much faster, but produce little thrust for their weight. Aerospikes, a sort of inside-out rocket motor, offer better low altitude performance, but have weight and cooling issues. The litany of trade-offs was endless, and it often brought us around to his favorite design, the engine for the infamous Blackbird, the SR-71 spyplane.

"Look at this," he said in one early session. He'd chalked out what looked like a drainpipe with a jet engine inside one end and a cone projecting from the other. "The ram moves out of the way at low speed so the turbojet can operate, then at supersonic speeds, diverts most of the flow into the afterburner. Now that's a hybrid — the world's first turbo-ramjet!"

The engine was complex, with all kinds of flaps and doors and ducts to adjust its operation in flight, and it was no orbital booster. But with 1950's technology, it could fly from a dead stop on the runway clear to the edge of space. It thrilled Mr. Coanda to no end, and learning it all kept me busy while I adapted to the loss of my mother.

My lessons weren't all theoretical, though. We went on launching rockets in the pattern of his Russian design. He called them sounding rockets and fitted them with nacelles and windows to test his ideas, and electronics to record the results. In an effort to attain higher speeds, he once had me lash a rocket to a set of weather balloons so it could fire toward the ground from 70,000 feet. He got the data he needed, but made a four foot crater in the woods behind the garden. We never did that again.

Through a former colleague, Mr. Coanda had access to a laser sintering machine that could print computer-designed components direct into high-performance alloys. It was the highlight of my summer when he took me into town to see it work. Through a quartz observation window, we watched as metallic traces appeared in a bed of power, then were buried one after the other by a mechanical sweeping wand.

Each trace added a sliver of substance to an emerging whole, but not until the process finished and the dust was dug away could I see the arrayed components of what was clearly a new, more complex, second stage for his rocket. This one was a hybrid of old and new. Instead of a solid rocket motor core, it would be liquid fueled, and instead of a conventional rocket, there was a pointed cone threaded to screw into the duct where the nozzle should be.

From his lectures, I knew what that meant. "It's an aerospike engine!" Mr. Coanda tapped the side of his nose. "It's a clue. It still needs a first stage booster, but with thrust from the spike and the ramjet together, I reckon it can pass Mach 5. That's fast enough, I need Ralph here to coat the leading edges with ceramic to keep them from melting." He gave a nod to the lab-coated technician who'd been operating the machine.

Ralph was a tidy, redheaded man with a neatly-trimmed goatee. "It's your money," he said. "Come on son, help me wrap up these parts."

Before we could put Coanda's investment to the test, we first had to resuscitate a tiny liquid oxygen plant moldering behind his workshop. He'd built it before he retired, "tinkered it together" he said, from a helicopter engine and an assortment of modified turbocompressor parts. Liquid air, he explained, is made by successively compressing, cooling, and expanding air until it fractions into liquid components. It requires heavy industrial machinery to produce in bulk, but he thought it should be possible to use jet engine technology to compress the process into something light enough to carry along on a booster.

"And it works terrific," he said, "It'll never produce enough LOX to do the whole job alone, but that's another trade-off. If it can do much better than pay its own way, then—"

"You don't need as big a rocket."

He winked. "Exactly, and it works out that to get the LOX, you also produce a large volume of super-cold nitrogen that can help with cooling. If you then find a use for the super-heated waste air, say to insulate your combustion surfaces, it might make a serious contribution to a more efficient booster."

We got the plant working and collected enough liquid oxygen to test fire the engine. Ralph — Mr. Phillips at the fabrication shop — had given the spike a standard baked-on ceramic coating to protect it from hot rocket exhaust, but it immediately became clear that when the engine was throttled to full power, this essential protection just crumbled away. This was serious, but Mr. Coanda took it in stride. Testing proceeded. The print run had included spare parts, so he just swapped out the spike cones as they eroded. That was enough for some low power tests, and gave him the data he needed to return to his computerized drawing board.

While he refined his design ideas, I pursued one of my own. If we could get a machine to lay down metal alloy a few atoms at a time, I thought, maybe we could coax it to blend in some silica and print the heat shield right into the components. I paid Ralph Phillips a visit and bent his arm by telling him the experiments I needed were for the science fair.

First we tried printing a simple flat washer and used a service probe to drop a pinch of silica into its upper surface. It worked okay until the machine cooled down. Then Mr. Phillips fished out the washer with tongs and set it under an articulated magnifier lamp. "I was afraid of that," he said, "Your idea worked, but the materials have different coefficients of expansion." He slid to the side to let me look through the magnifier. The coating was crazed like an old master's painting.

He ran his fingers through his shabby goatee. "I have a book here...somewhere..." He rummaged through his desk, then the adjoining office, until he found what he was looking for. "You want a science fair project? This book contains everything they learned making tiles for the space shuttle and then some. Some of it's too complex for us to do here, but if you can think up a way to do it in this machine, I'll order the materials and let you burn it, within reason. You make it work, and you can write your own ticket. What do you say?"

I could hardly say no. That summer, we ran over sixty tests, enough I thought I'd surely overstayed my welcome. The solution finally came in the fall, with blending the margin between the metal and silica, then doping the layers with scandium and zirconium dioxide to improve their bonding and strength. To do all this, Mr. Phillips had to consult with a physicist for advice, and bolt a hand-made silica hopper inside the cabinet of the very expensive sintering machine. When we finally got it all to work, all we really had to show for our effort was a shiny black disk of metal. But we had built the hopper just big enough and just tricked out enough to make Mr. Coanda's aerospike.

After Momma died, I'd taken on a couple of her tutoring students and that had grown into a regular job. Between that and my time in the fabrication shop, I hadn't been to Mr. Coanda's much since spring. I knew he had test fired a ducted aerospike engine meant for first stage liftoff and two disappointing scramjet hybrids he hoped would serve at higher speeds and altitudes. I knew what he was doing. He hoped to achieve a single stage to orbit by building a tunable air and LOX breathing super-hybrid engine. He didn't have the resources to build and test it as a single functioning unit, so he was breaking it down and testing the various flight modes it would have to support, just like the Wright brothers had done.

I didn't go immediately to show him the new spike cone. Saturday was his birthday and Daddy had invited him over for cake and a movie on our new giant screen. I bought a nice gift box, wrapped up the spike like a Fabergé egg, and tied it up in a bow. Saturday came, then the appointed time. The kitchen filled with sounds of cooking and then with tidying and cleaning. But instead of the rumble of Mr. Coanda's pickup I heard the bleat of my phone from the bedroom. At the other end was Ralph Phillips, from the shop.

"Jim?"

"Yes sir?"

"Jim, have you seen George lately?"

"George? Oh, No sir, I—"

"He was in here today with a file I've already printed for him twice, that first one you two tested last year. Big burns like these are expensive, and when I asked about it, he blew up at me — acted like he didn't know what I was talking about. We go back a long way, me and George. I'd do anything for him, but I'm worried."

My heart sank. I'd already seen the signs: the duplicate subscriptions and purchases, the forgotten experiments, the tendency to put me in charge of things beyond my age and experience. I'd thought he was just pushing me. I'd hoped that was all, but I'd known better. Now I knew I had to say something and I worried, after the call, just how he'd react.

Daddy said he'd go with me. I told him to finish the cake, then drove my little Volkswagen over to Mr. Coanda's with the gift-wrapped aerospike and a sack of pecans Daddy had collected from our trees out back. When I climbed Mr. Coanda's steps, it was as if for the last time. I noticed how the porch had grown crowded with neglected pots, how the algae-green boards had crumbled from its edge, how the screen door screeched when the spring slammed it shut behind me.

Mr. Coanda was in his study, a tiny room off the kitchen that in most houses built in the thirties and added on to over the years, might have been a bedroom or larder.

"Come in here, James. Put that down."

In all the years I'd known him, he'd never called me James. He sat in the plain leather office chair Daddy'd bought him when the wicker came out of the old one. The computer glowed by the open window, on the little wooden desk he always said had been made for a typewriter. The bigger table, a big drafting board he mostly left locked flat to serve as a workbench, was strewn with plans and papers. He tossed a few more into this mix and rested his elbows on the table edge.

I stepped up to the table, resisting the urge to straighten. Some of the papers were receipts from the fabrication shop going back over a year.

His eyes glistened. His voice was low and flat. "I yelled at Ralph today."

"You're just slowing down, that's all."

"Don't patronize me, boy! You think I'm so far gone I can't see where I'm standing?" He smacked the table hard enough to nudge it out of level. His outburst struck like a physical blow. In all the time I'd known him, he'd never once raised his voice.

He frowned and stared at the table, then turned in his chair. Behind the keyboard, he had two bottles of Nehi. He popped one open and handed it to me. Grape scent mixed with the woodsy breeze through the window. "I'm not talking about a little tremor, Jimmy, or forgetting where I keep the wasp spray."

Several times I'd had to remind him that, in the time I had known him, it had always been in the kitchen, and not the washroom as he often remembered.

He stretched to drop the opener in a drawer and the floor made a loud creak. He looked down, but instead of commenting on the noise said, "I used to stay on top of things. I used to..."

His long fingers worked around the neck of his bottle like they didn't quite know what to do with it.

"Have you ridden along the fence line lately, like you and your brother used to do?"

"No sir."

"The other day, I found a meth lab hid out in the woods there..." He had started to point through the window and say, "just out past the pecan tree." I'd heard this story before, and it wasn't "the other day." He took a quick sip and set the bottle back down, cradling it between his hands. "I've outlived it all, Jimmy. My dreams, this place, and finally the old noggin. Not much left after that." I looked up, but he spoke before I could say anything. "And don't say nothing about heaven. You know I don't believe that hooey. And anyway, after a man's lost his marbles, even St. Peter can't cram 'em back inside, and nobody can tell me different." He took another sip.

"It's going," he said, tapping his fingers against his forehead, "and when it's gone, it's gone, that's all. The flame has to pass to you." He turned and looked out the window. "I'd have loved to have made it to the moon, though," he said, "returned the dust inside these bones to the stars from which it came."

He swiveled back around. His eyes found tear marks on my cheek. "Don't misunderstand me, boy."

"Sir?"

"You don't owe me anything. I didn't teach you all this so you could finish my life's work."

"It's good work."

He smiled and sipped his Nehi. "Damn straight it's good work. And good work always gets done by somebody or other — when the time is right. No, I taught you because that's all I had to pass on. You're welcome to carry on where I left off if that's your passion. If it ain't, though, don't do it because it was mine. Every man has to follow his own dreams, Jimmy. Wherever yours lead you, I'm proud of you, and your pa's proud."

He set down the empty with a clunk. "What's that?" He was looking at the present, still cradled in my hand.

"It's...for your birthday."

"My...but that was.... Open it for me, will you?" I opened it. I pulled off the ribbon and the lid and set it on the desk before him with the wrappings drawn aside. He stared down and reached his hand to turn the box.

He pinched the cone by its edges and held it up to the light. "Remarkable." He tapped his nail against the impervious surface. "Tell me all about it."

I told him.

"Well that's as fine a science fair project as I believe I'm likely to see," he said. "You *do* have a project, don't you?"

"Um...yessir." I had all the data, anyway.

Rain started pattering against the window sill. He rose to lower the sash. "We were going to have cake."

"Yessir."

He smiled. "Drive me over. Come back early, and we'll put your spike on the ducted first stage and see how it flies. If I remember my own name in the morning."

The science fair project carried me to state, then to international, then through a whirlwind of dinners and photo ops. I had a job if I wanted one, before I'd even applied to college. I needed a broader grounding, though, so I headed for Stanford and four years of internship at Lockheed and Rocketdyne. In April of my senior year, my intern manager at Rocketdyne, Rob Curtis, approached me about a start-up that wanted to build a single stage to orbit engine using venture capital instead of waiting for government contracts. He said they knew about my science fair win, and if I was interested, he'd come along and help me assemble a team. I said I'd think about it and flew home for the break, eager to get some advice.

Keith's recovery had drawn him to medicine and to Austin. He had married my junior year. Daddy was there fawning over his new grandson, but before I joined them, I wanted to see Mr. Coanda. We'd spent less and less time together as his world contracted and my own life narrowed towards college. After the birthday blow up, he'd hired a caregiver service and Daddy had started keeping tabs on him. I still worried, though. I'd kept up a correspondence, even after his replies tailed off, and whenever I came home, I'd mow his grass or fix whatever was broken or help him to shell some pecans. The last year, he seldom spoke or gave any indication he knew me, but he seemed happy enough for the company.

I flew home and hailed a cab, but as soon as it pulled up at the end of that winding driveway, I knew he was gone. I knew the same way you know when the power's out in the middle of the night — by the relative amplification of trifles. Sorghum was sprouting in the feeders. A dog's bark echoed from beyond the darkened house without so much as a squeaking floorboard or singing water pipe to mute it. The door was unlocked, the rooms empty, except for a few chipped dishes and mounds of rubbish and clothing. Barest of all was the office. Everything was gone, a lifetime's worth of dreams condensed onto paper and computer files and finally all swept away.

The wind chuffed up around the eaves and loosed a hail of acorns across the roof. A clank echoed in through the window glass and I saw that the barn had collapsed. It was as if the place had been holding its breath, and now that he was gone, had given in to decades of overdue entropy.

I ran outside, tears on my face, and looked for Mr. Coanda's rockets, his motors, his tools — but everything was gone. Nothing remained but a few ruined bags of cement and the odd bit of wire or tail fin.

Down the hill, the workshop sat padlocked and empty. The only thing left of Mr. Coanda's was the cryo-plant out back. The power was out, or I might have cranked it like I had two years ago when I'd found him gripping the tarp, refusing to be led back inside.

"Start," he'd said when I pulled at his elbow.

He turned and looked with a little vigor in his eye. "Start," he said again, his grip still firm on the tarpaulin.

I didn't think it was a good idea, mechanically speaking, but it seemed best to play along. "It's been sitting a long time. The injectors might be fouled."

He made a dismissive noise. "Natural gas, ain't it? Start her up. I wanna hear her." I grabbed the filthy canvas, careful of the mildew, and pulled it out of the way. With the fuel and compressor valves properly set, I turned the key. The little turbojet engine spun up, tinkitty-tink like cards on the spokes of a bicycle wheel until the centripetal force built enough to splay the compressor blades into their hangers. Then the pip, pip, pip of the igniter sparks till the flame caught and the compressors roared to life. With the growing cacophony, there returned a little of the rocket man I'd so long admired. He smiled and gripped my shoulder and started shouting over the machine, telling me about its operation like a kid just back from his first circus. Then he fiddled with the controls as if performing some procedure unknown to me, and finally throttled down and closed the fuel valve.

As the plant whirred down to a stop, he looked at me and back at it and back at me again.

"Jimmy." It was a question, but his eyes shown with recognition.

"Yessir."

He poked my sternum with his finger. "You won the Science Fair."

"Yessir."

He wrapped me in a bear hug and patted my back a few times. "I'm so proud of you boy. So proud..."

And that was that. He stood back, his eyes gray and distant, and ambled up the path towards the nurse, who'd run down from the house at our racket.

And now the same house sat empty, as if in appointment with doom.

There was a note on Daddy's door. I called and got a Mr. Callahan, an estate lawyer who was eager to meet me — immediately if at all possible. It was a quarter till midnight when the yard filled with headlights turning off from the highway and then the squeaking clatter of Mr. Coanda's pickup. My heart jumped at the familiar sound, but of course it was only the lawyer. It seemed Mr. Coanda had arranged a reverse mortgage with a developer eager to have the property. The lawyer asked for my id, then had me stand in the light for comparison. Then he exchanged my signature for a sealed manila envelope. Inside was a note in Mr. Coanda's arrhythmic hand:

"My dear boy, Jimmy.

I'm having a few things packed up for you to have after I'm gone. It's surprising, when it comes to it, how easy a lifetime can fit in a box, but remember what I told you. The flame isn't in the box, it's in you. Wherever it leads, there's sure to be light."

It was dated the year I started college.

The lawyer waited till I looked up, then said, "You're meant to have the truck as well." He walked around to the tailgate and pulled back a shiny blue tarp to reveal the crate from out in the barn. "Mr. Coanda left explicit instructions," he said, "and I carried them out to the letter, but Jesus..."

He lifted the lid from the crate enough to expose the odd Russian missile, complete with Soviet insignia and olive green livery. The foam blocks had been disturbed, and the resulting spaces packed with paper files and blueprint tubes and a plastic bag full of thumb drives.

The lawyer was as pale as the moonlight. "I don't know what you two were cooking up and I'm pretty sure I don't want to. But I was afraid what might happen if someone found this, so I've had it in my garage for safe keeping."

I looked again at the note. Below his signature, Mr. Coanda had added a postscript: "There will be a manifest with this note. If he breaks anything important, don't tell him the missiles are fake."

I laughed, a good parting joke between friends. Then I fed Mr. Callahan pizza and drove him home to his family.

The Texas gulf sky is broadly chalked with crisscrosses of coral and cobalt. I wait by the hatch, mentally ticking off the others as they shuffle up the companionway and step aboard the nameless craft that will carry us up into orbit. Mists issue below, hissing from between eight tall nacelles ringing the gourd-like vessel, with engines still silent beneath their tall, black ram-cones. A service truck backs away and turns along the low earthen berm erected to protect neighboring pads from any debris thrown up by our departure. Beyond the berms and the terminal and the palm-lined fence, headlights speed south along the highway from Refugio.

In the old days, I used to drive Anna that way, south and then west into the nature preserve to watch the sunset. We'd have the chaise lounges in the truck bed, and we'd lay out eating strawberries and counting satellites and dreaming of days to come. We were fresh out of school, new to the world. We didn't know what dreams could be till we tangled our lives together.

That first full scale engine took six years and fourteen engineers, materials scientists, and propulsion specialists. It was complex and heavy, but it made up for it with all the right trade-offs. It was basically Coanda's super-hybrid, but with an air-breathing gas turbine added to power the propellant pumps and an on-board cryo plant based on the one behind his workshop. The shroud used to direct combustion gases down along the aerospike also formed part of the duct. At liftoff, it gulped huge quantities of air to be shot out as reaction mass. At higher speeds, a ram moved up and fuel was injected to form a ramjet, the geometry of which continuously varied to produce thrust up to fifteen times the speed of sound. The onboard cryo-plant supplied LOX to the aerospike and super-cold nitrogen to cool the engine and intake air during hypersonic flight. As in the SR-71, a complex arrangement of vents, rams, and bypass tubes tuned the engine to changes in altitude and speed. Even the trajectory was a trade-off, an s-shaped compromise between the ballistic flight of a conventional missile and the long flat climb of a spaceplane.

Overall, the atmosphere supplied twenty percent of the reaction mass and half the oxygen at liftoff. The first test vehicle was a third lighter than a comparable conventional booster, and with the impregnated thermal protection I had helped pioneer, it could fly again and again. The stats only improved from there.

Now here I am, at the door to the fruits of our labors. I duck inside the cabin and climb to the loft, where I slide onto a fabric web couch. Launch attendants squeeze around us, cinching harnesses and telling jokes and patting my shoulder like a charm.

The hatch closes. I clap three times to attract everyone's attention before the gab can get started.

"Listen."

The turbines are spinning up, eight whirring voices that sing in beating cascades till the roar finally chokes their harmonics.

The bulkhead display screens flash a recorded prelaunch briefing, but I don't pay much attention. My thoughts wander back to Coanda, back to our shared dreams of space-born adventure, of ray-guns and moon walks and daredevil launches on towers of billowing flame. Funny how time can shift the weights of all the things we treasure.

Single stage to orbit, reusable spacecraft made space travel less Neil Armstrong than George Jetson. It opened the door to a new space economy, and here we were in South Texas, further south than Cape Kennedy, with a clear shot over the gulf and easy highway access to the whole of the continent, from Matamoros to Port Huron. By the time Lockheed Propulsion made the buyout offer, Refugio was set to be the LAX of a new age, and we, its founding elite. The future came rushing headlong, but we were happily settled with a house outside Corpus and daughters in school and a love for kayaking the wilds of the marshes and bays along the coast.

We bankrolled the money. I went to work on the Refugio spaceport, Anna for the start-ups that sprang up around it like dandelions. Now they're planning spaceports on the Yucatan peninsula and Brazil's Atlantic coast, and our eldest is building a third in Northern Queensland. I have grand kids in California and Germany, and camping buddies with aerospace jobs south of the border. Space is the new frontier, but it's still warm and green on the good Earth, and the moon's not the siren she once was.

Which is not to say I won't enjoy the ride. I'm as eager as anyone to play in micro-gravity and drag my booted toes in the lunar regolith. I'll ride over to the Sea of Tranquility and take all the souvenir photos, and I might even dream a floating monolith before I fly back home to Anna. But it's not wanderlust that drives me up through the azure Texas night. Nor is it pride or national prestige, nor even George Coanda's triple-fired, vacuum-packed, anti-static treated cinerary remains that have waited forty years to be laid to rest in the only fitting spot I can imagine.

No, I'm here for the kids, eight of my fellow travelers who are my guests at Camp Kitty-Hawk, where for twenty years we've brought students from around the world to use science and engineering to break down and realize their dreams. Each year we invite proposals for a different field of study. There's always an extended field trip, but only now is the infrastructure in place to allow for a trip to the moon.

George would be thrilled. He'd listen to the snickering and the false bravado and the rude jokes and noises, and he'd smile the way he always did when it wasn't yet time to speak. They're excited to be going. They think it's cool, but they don't yet have an inkling of the trade-offs and sacrifices that have gotten mankind this far. That's exactly what they're here to learn.

The murmuring resumes. One of the girls says to another, "Shhh! The Rocket Man will hear you."

I've run the camp now for longer than I worked in engineering, but to these kids and the world, I'll always be the Rocket Man, a mythological hero from a golden age. And that's fine by me. I'll proudly wear that title while I fan the flames, till the next bearer comes along to change up the world behind me. It's not the adventure I imagined for my life, but you never quite know where dreams will lead.

C. Stuart Hardwick is a Writers of the Future winner, a Jim Baen Memorial Award winner, and a James White award semifinalist. He's a regular in *Analog Science Fiction & Fact*, and his work has appeared in *Galaxy's Edge*, *Andromeda Spaceways In-Flight Magazine*, *Forbes.com* and *Mental Floss*, among others.

A southerner from South Dakota, Stuart grew up creating "radio" dramas and stop-action animated shorts before moving on to ill-conceived flying machines. He worked with the creators of the video game Doom, married an aquanaut, and trained his dog to pull a sled. He's been known to wear a cape.

For more info and a free e-sampler, visit www.cStuartHardwick.com.

Möbius

First published in Nature 515,304 (November 2014)

J.W. Alden

I've watched you die a thousand times.

The first was the hardest. I watched the birds from my hotel balcony, tracing every arc and dive, marking each wire they touched, each windowsill. If one of them hadn't landed on the stoplight above you, I might never have noticed you crossing the street. I might never have noticed the van, a blurry streak of silver barreling your way.

Your first death was the hardest, but it was the most beautiful. I had to see it again.

Chaos touches those around you, extending outward like ripples in a pond. The birds scatter into the air. A man walking his dog on the sidewalk drops his leash. A woman three paces behind you stumbles backward with hands over her mouth. Teenagers huddled around a nearby storefront reach for cellphones, one to dial 9-1-1, the others to snap pictures.

The look in your eyes never changes, that sudden dilation just before fluttering to a close. They shimmer like starlight, even as your head snaps back and auburn wisps tangle in the windshield wipers.

The driver's name is Will. He's forty-two. He has a wife and a daughter. He told me over a cup of coffee at the bar he'd been in that afternoon. He seemed nice. Not the killing type, I think. But a conversation won't change what happens, no matter how many times we have it. This last time, we talked about God and destiny and drunk driving, just before the quantum beacon beneath my rib cage came to life and brought me to the beginning again, as it always does.

It's not Will's fault. He's a slave to this moment, entangled. Like you. Like me.

They told me this could happen. Over the years, I heard stories of beacons blinking out, operatives lost. Never the whos, whens, or whys, only that it's happened before and will happen again. I shrugged away those warnings, certain I'd never get caught up in extracurricular voyeurism. Tracking the H7N9 mutation was too important. Or so I believed then.

But the mission grows stale. I'm weary of chasing birds, watching money change hands. I observe the same moments again and again, unable to do anything but watch, learn, report. Just once, I want change. *Permanent* change that won't be erased when the beacon chimes and the machines bring me home for a pat on the head—or back to the start for another try. They keep saying the government will let us prevent the outbreak one day. But we've been at this for years, and it's clear we're just going to keep watching. We're not the heroes they said we'd be. We're just filling in the history books.

I don't know what it is about you, your death, your moment. But the first time I called out and you looked up as the silver streak took you, pointed your chin in a slightly different direction than the previous hundred times, I knew I'd never free myself of this.

I tried to learn your name once. You scowled, unaware of the favor I'd done you. Silver drifted by, your fragile form unassailed. It didn't matter. My interval expired, and the beacon chimed. I woke again in that hotel, across from that intersection, ready to watch you die or not die for the thousandth time.

It will go on like this until I can accept the futility of it. I can weigh your fate again and again, or I can turn away, carry out my task in your time, and make my report—leaving you, Will, and all the others forever at the mercy of this moment.

I've seen it from every angle now. Each time, I come closer to doing what must be done. Each time, I wonder how long they'll let me do this. They must have drilled this scenario. There must be some contingency. Maybe the next time my beacon goes off, I'll wake with a bright light in my face, people in lab coats and army uniforms asking how many tries it takes to find one lousy bird. Or maybe I'll just keep going, on and on, until I decide I'm done.

At the very least, my suspicions have been confirmed, one death at a time. It's not about you. Never was. We cling to each heartbeat, each fleeting moment, desperate to make use before they're gone. But I've found one I can have and hold, one I can love and abuse and make my own. Maybe even one I can change.

You? You just happen to be there for it.

I'm not sure why you smile this time. Maybe it's the way the sun hits my shoulders. Maybe it's the bounce in my step as I cross the street.

For the first time since the first time, I realize how unaware you are of this moment we're caught in. You don't know about Will. You don't know about the dropped dog leash or the camera phones. You don't know that I've saved your life again and again, that I've let you die a thousand times. You also don't know how the beacon works or what a piezoelectric power source is. You don't know that it will cease to function when my heart stops beating.

Your smile fades when I wrap my hands around your shoulders. A trembled shout leaves your lips as I shove you backward onto the sidewalk. I mouth a silent apology for robbing you of this moment as I step into the path of the van. Your eyes grow wide, but it's not the starry shimmer I notice this time; it's the silver streak within.

J.W. Alden is a 1st Place Writers of the Future winner, a graduate of Odyssey Writing Workshop, and an active member of SFWA. His fiction has appeared in *Nature*, *Daily Science Fiction*, *Flash Fiction Online*, and various other publications

Growing up along the coasts of Florida, he learned to love the shade. He now lives in Philadelphia, Pennsylvania, where he is trying desperately to understand the difference between a state and a commonwealth.

More at www.authoralden.com

Rats Will Run

First published in Mirror Shards Volume Two (2012)

Marina J. Lostetter

I freaking hate rats. So I couldn't, for the life of me, figure out why Pedro wanted to release a test group in the lab. "Can't you do it in the observation cube? Why in here? They'll get their rat germs all over everything." I shivered, thinking about my tablet with tiny paw prints scattered across it.

"No, no. It has to be in here," he insisted, pushing up his thick-framed glasses. "Gabby, trust me, you want to see this. I discovered it by accident." Taking off with a hop and a skip, he went to retrieve a set of cages.

"Accident? What does that mean? One got loose? Geez, man, I had my lunch sitting out here yesterday."

He let out a disturbing, manic cackle.

Perhaps he'd finally snapped — gone stir-crazy. We'd had a handful go wiggy over the past year. One guy even went outside the base sans pressure-suit. That wasn't pretty. Isolation can do that to people — and it was hard to get more isolated than HD 10180-4.

We liked to call the planet Cit-Bolon-Tum (Tums for short), after one of the Mayan gods of medicine. It offered thousands of curative prospects, which was why all two hundred base-dwellers had made the trek to its shores.

"Is this what our Saturday nights have come to?" I asked as he hefted two cages — each with three rats — onto one of the touch-tables. "Oh, come on, I have to give presentations with that."

"You can use the far wall," he said, rolling his eyes. "How did you get into bio-research if you hate animals so much?"

"Microbiology," I specified. "Microorganisms. You know, the things that don't have faces. Or claws, or whiskers, or long, naked tails."

"You still have to run experiments. Cancer cells don't exist in a vacuum."

I shrugged. The teasing from my subordinates was routine. I was the only biologist on the team — to hear them talk, *in all of mankind* — that hated nature. Well, not all of it. Just anything that scurried, or crawled, or scuttled. Which applied to almost all of Cit-Bolon-Tum's complex life-forms.

"Get to it," I insisted. "What's this great rat-discovery you've made?"

"Watch," he said with a giggle. "These ones on the left have been given compound 0697. The ones on the right are the control group." He opened one cage, then the other, pulling a rat from each. Proudly, he held up both — a little grandstanding. Then, he turned both loose on the floor.

I leapt up onto a stool near the counter, almost knocking over an irreplaceable electron microscope in the process.

One rat went left, the other right.

I was less than impressed. "So—"

"Not done." He did the same with the remaining rats. All of those who'd been injected with 0697 ran to the same corner. The control group scampered willy-nilly.

"Uh… Ok."

"Did you see?"

"Come on, Pedro. What? Did you put something in that corner, and only the test group can smell it, or—"

"No, you weren't watching." He went over to the touch-wall, and I retrieved a pair of glasses from my lab coat's breast pocket. "Wall, on," he commanded. "Lab six ceiling feed. Replay last five minutes."

"I don't need to watch it again, I—"

As the surveillance feed replayed, he marked each rat with a number by tapping the wall. "Trace paths of all subjects, from twenty-four seconds through four minutes and thirty eight seconds. Give me real-space lines."

The wall displayed each rat's path as a different color. When Pedro put both hands on the wall the image stuck to them. He tore the picture away and threw it at the room, where the digital lines settled on the floor.

The control group had drawn a series of squirrely lines — like a toddler given a crayon for the first time. The tested rats drew one line — a perfectly straight diagonal towards the corner. So straight as to be clearly unnatural.

I removed my glasses to rub my eyes, and the room-overlay disappeared from view. "Ok, what does that mean?"

"They're following something we can't detect. There's something there that the compound helps them find."

"Weird, I admit, but I'm not sure... What are you going on about? Not *that* again?"

He shrugged, casually strolled over the lab door, and *opened it*.

I jumped to my feet. "What are you doing?"

"I want to see where they go." The test group hurried out, as though drawn by an invisible piper.

"Not cool, man," I said. Pedro *tried* to follow the rats, but I grabbed him by the coat-sleeve. "You going to let them into my apartment next? This is a gag, isn't it? Who put you up to this?"

With a smile and a shake of his head, he brushed me off. "No, Gabby. Pure science, honest." And he jogged after his new friends.

Thankfully the rodents weren't interested in the base's sleeping quarters. They ran through the white-walled halls (once pristine, now covered in doodles the residents dared call 'art'), towards the eastern airlock. Strangely, they followed the same diagonal they had in the lab, changing halls and rounding corners only when they couldn't stay directly on the line.

Once they hit the hyper-glass airlock doors they stopped. Rising up on their hind legs, little noses twitching, they pawed at the door-seal like dogs begging to be let outside.

I looked through the four layers of glass to the dangerous beauty that was Tums' surface. Dramatic hills and sharp mountains made up the majority of the land, creating a terrain more rolling and varied than anything I'd seen on Earth. Life butted right up to the outside of the base in the form of low, jungle-like foliage — most of which was mobile, meaning the scene outside changed constantly. Nothing on the planet stood more than three feet high, so despite the up-and-down of the terrain, we could look for miles before hitting the craggy horizon.

"Oh, look, they want outside," I said, throwing as much sing-song into my tone as I could. "We just need to get them into their little ratty spacesuits and they can keep playing blood-hound. Oh, wait." I slapped the side of my face. "Rats don't have spacesuits."

"Ha-ha," Pedro said, scratching his chin.

I patted him on the shoulder. "Sorry, dude. Guess today's pursuit of directed panspermia ends here."

A very girly — though distinctly male — shriek emanated from several halls over. "Better go round up your other pets," I said. "Or else I won't be the only one raining on your free-range parade."

"But, they're *drawn* to something, aren't you interested in what?"

I crossed my arms. "Not in the slightest."

Head hung low, he scampered off to collect the rats, and I made a note to keep an eye on his mental health.

It seemed like there was at least one panspermia nut in every lab I'd ever worked in. The discovery of extraterrestrial life just over a century before I was born ignited a blaze of new believers. I had no problem with the basic theory — that life down here could have come from out there. It was the *Seeders* I took issue with. Those crystal waving, *we-couldn't-have-built-the-pyramids-without-em* shouting, pseudo-scientific doofuses. The guys that thought intelligent ETs guided our evolution.

I was so sad when Pedro proved to be one of them. And he was always looking for any oddity, any abnormality he could point to and say, "Look, this might mean extraterrestrial intelligence was here!"

I had no interest in hearing what he thought the rat-march meant.

After thoroughly searching my quarters to make sure they were furry-intruder free, I settled down for the evening. Though the planet had roughly sixteen-hour days, we ran on Earth time, and it was nearing one in the morning. Sure, the off-set time felt strange when occasionally it was pitch-black out at two in the afternoon, but otherwise it was easier to follow home. After all, we rarely left base. Kind host Cit-Bolon-Tum decidedly was not.

At three in the morning I got a pound on my door and a muffled entreaty. "Mendoza? Dr. Mendoza, are you in there?"

Groggy and slightly pissed, I kicked away the covers, threw on a shirt and went to the door. "What is it?" I said through the comm. box.

"Someone from your team has taken an un-authorized surface walk."

"What? How do you know it's one of us?" I could tell it was Sammy — oh, *excuse* me, Dr. Slavitz — on the other side of the door. Damn formal bastard. "Bet it's one of your sickle-cell lackeys. Why's cancer always getting the blame for base problems?"

"It's one of your suits that's missing. Inventory already confirmed."

"Great," I said to myself before yanking open the door. "Who haven't you found yet?"

"Doctors Smith, Cohen, and Alvarez are yet unaccounted for."

"Then I know who it is."

"Pedro?"

"I told you, he's not talking—"

"Shut it, Slavits."

A hoard of us had shuffled into the communications room. I let up on the output button, hoping he'd respond via his suit's system. I knew he could hear me.

"Dude, it's Gabriella. If you tell me there's a rat in that suit with you I'm not letting you back on the base, *ever*."

A brief moment of static, then, "Better, Gabby. Even better."

The whole room let out a collective sigh. Myself excluded.

"What's that mean, 'better'? Huh?"

"I injected myself with 0697."

My nails curled against the control panel. All chatter in the room fell dead. "You're shitting me."

"You should see this. It's amazing!"

Slavitz leaned over my shoulder. "He's another one. Shut in here too long — he cracked. We need to get him to Dr. Nakamura."

As much as I hated agreeing with the prick, he was right. Pedro needed a little brain-blending.

"You've gotta come back in, Pedro. We'll make an appointment with the shrink. You're tripping on the compound — you're hallucinating just like your rodents." Wishing I wasn't in a room full of eavesdroppers I said, "You know that crap isn't ready for human testing. We don't even know what it does to the rats yet."

"Seriously, Gabby, you have to—"

"Get your *ass* back to the airlock."

"But it's so wonderful..."

I tossed the microphone across the room, and the crowd backed away. "If the idiot won't come in alone, I'll drag him back myself."

"You can't go by yourself," said Slavits. "No fewer than five to a party."

"You volunteering? No? If we do things by the book he might step into a ground-mouth before we've even suited up — especially since he's hallucinating. I'll go out. If we both bite the big one, blame me in the report."

Other members of the cancer research team stepped forward, offering their assistance. "Sure," I said, grateful to have my team rallied, "But I'm not waiting for safety checks and all that garbage. I'm going now. If you all want to keep to protocol, no worries. Follow when you're ready."

After an arduous wrestling match with my pressure suit, I made it through the airlock and out into the twilight. Just my luck the jerk would have to go tromping around during the night cycle. I gave a wave to those inside, then headed down the paved foot-path towards port.

Moving on Tums was like trying to wade through quicksand. The hard skeleton of the suit was supposed to compensate for the planet's 1.9 gs, but frankly, it didn't. It let me lift my limbs a little easier, but did nothing for the ton-of-bricks feeling that dropped into my pants once I'd left the artificial environment of the base.

Outside for the first time in months, I let out a heavy sigh, which immediately fogged up the left side of my helmet. Stupid defogging film was supposed to be replaced every three weeks — those maintenance guys were slacking.

The front of the helmet acted like my lab glasses, displaying a whole set of new info and figures over my natural vision. Labels sprang up on various plants, detailing their primary composition and discovered uses. Air pressure figures and weather system stats scrolled across the top. Every time a plant or animal moved a blue line tracked its path (and made me ever-so-grateful to have layers of super durable materials between me and the critters). I blinked them all aside — keeping only the red arrow that pointed me down the paved path in Pedro's direction.

Each suit contained a homing beacon, so no one could get lost. Now eaten, decapitated, or punctured — those were a different matter. The planet had a million ways to kill a person, but at least we could always find what was left of their suit.

"Yo, amigo," I called, my voice sounding hollow in the helmet. "I'm out here. Waiting for you to show me this wow-awesome-totally-scientific-and-not-at-all-insane discovery you've made."

"I don't appreciate the sarcasm."

"And I don't appreciate being dragged out of my beauty sleep because some member of my team decided to go on an unauthorized walkabout." Each step reminded me just how out of shape I was. My scrawny build was not Cit-Bolon-Tum compatible.

"I don't have cabin fever, Gabby."

"Ok. Whatever."

"There are lines on the ground. Natural overlays."

"Will you at least agree to stay put until I find you?"

"Of course," he said. "Because you have to see this."

Forty minutes later we were reunited. But not happily. At least he hadn't left the path.

Little critters and plants had followed me off and on along the way, giving me the willies. A poisonous cephalopod — possessed of eight skinny legs instead of tentacles, whose fur-slime could eat through every layer of my suit — gave chase for a hundred yards before it decided easier prey lay elsewhere. I thought about getting out my aerosol tranqu-spray and gassing the sucker, but didn't want to waste it in case something bigger came along.

Ah, man, I'd spend twenty-four hours locked in a room filled with deadly fliangia spores if I never had to see a rodent-reminiscent creature again.

"What is your major malfunction?" I demanded when I turned a corner and found my subordinate crouching on the asphalt.

Pedro had his back to me and didn't turn around. He waved a gloved hand inches above the ground, as though stroking an invisible animal. "All green here, boss," he said, giving me a thumbs-up before going back to his air-petting.

No way was he right in the head. "Sure, you look as dandy as a dodo bird." I crossed my arms, peeved, when he gave no response. "Now tell me you were pulling my leg. Tell me one of my best technicians did not go kamikaze in the name of cancer research."

Compound 0697 came from the distillation and mixture of several animal secretions — animals all native to Cit-Bolon-Tum. And they each sported monikers that had something to do with death, acid, burning, maiming, etc. We'd hoped the compound — and many others like it — would specifically besiege cancer cells.

Now I had a feeling 0697 targeted healthy gray matter instead.

"I didn't do it for cancer," he said, turning in my direction, his movement slow and deliberate. "There's something out here."

His visor was up, giving me full access to the manic expression plastered across his face. Pupils dilated to the size of saucers, mouth twitching, small dribble of snot leaking from a nose he couldn't wipe

— I'd seen that expression before. But it wasn't exclusively the mask of *crazy*; it was also the look of breakthrough discovery.

But, since he was alone in a man-devouring environment, following invisible lines, and had previously stuck himself with a needle full of cell-destroying chemicals…

"Ok, well, how about we go back to base for now, eh?" I suggested. "We'll get a team together and come back at a reasonable hour."

"No can do, Gabby. You go back for a team," he said, turning away, "I'll stay."

No, uh-uh. No off-his-rocker techie was going to talk back to me. "That's it, mister." Crouching, I curled an arm through his, ready to haul him to his feet. In the next instant I yanked hard. The suit's skeleton not only helped in high gravity, but was also supposed to help me lift twice what I could naturally.

It would have worked if Pedro hadn't had the same equipment. Since he was a good size man and I had the scrawny build of a twelve-year-old boy, I wasn't going to win any battles of brute streng

But I gave it a five minute go anyway.

"Pedro, I swear, if you don't come back with me this instant I'm going to recommend you go into deepfreeze. I'll put you on a return shuttle and Earth can decide if they want to thaw you out again."

"Nice try, Gabby. Go back. I know what I'm doing. I want you to see it, but I'll go on alone. It's ok." Shifting fluidly, he stood up. I felt like a kid in an oversized mascot-costume, and he moved as if the suit were a second skin. He walked away from me, down the path.

"But…but what about guillotine vines?" I shouted. No need to raise my voice, of course, but I couldn't help it. "And ground-mouths?"

"I'll keep my eyes open." He gave a casual wave of his arm.

"Damn you, guys," I said, switching channels to speak to the base. "Wasn't I supposed to get backup?"

"I'm sorry, Dr. Mendoza," Slavits replied. "But a shark-cat's been stalking around the east entrance for a half an hour. We haven't seen its posse, but where there's one—"

"So just come out the north entrance and circle around." Dumbass. We had two airlocks for a reason.

"Love to…but it's jammed."

Well, hell. "Tell everyone on the maintenance crew they've officially made my shit-list."

With that I switched back to Pedro's channel and stumbled after him. If I wanted his ass saved I'd have to do it myself.

"Ok, dude. You win, for now. Tell me about these things you're seeing."

He had his hands out in front of him, like a blind man feeling his way. "The lines," he said softly, nearly a whisper, "They glow. And pulse, and shift — a stream of light."

"Uh-huh. And these lines, they just happened to follow the man-made path?" I raised an eyebrow. I had him there.

"No, it runs like this." He made a sweeping motion from northeast to southwest. "The path intersects it in some places. And it runs right through the base."

"And it's straight? Perfectly straight?"

"So far."

I called up a map of the area on my helmet's overlay and with my eyes drew the line he'd indicated. It wouldn't be long before the path and the line permanently diverged.

"And there's another set of lines over that way." He said, pointing yards off. "Going almost the same direction. I think it's angled slightly different."

The foliage to my right shook violently. I edged in closer to Pedro. "And you're following the line because…?"

"Because it leads somewhere."

"Right, and how do you know that?"

"Because of the flow. I told you, it's shifting like a stream — and I'm getting caught up in the current. It pulls me, just like the rats."

"You're talking in circles, bud."

"I know you're not a fan of my beliefs, Gabby. But I think what I'm looking at is proof. It's like a digital overlay — an augmentation — just like the displays in our helmets and in the labs. Only it's built right into the biology of Cit-Bolon-Tum. It's augmented reality on a chemical-induced level. Molecular computing — interfacing directly with the brain."

"Molecular computing? No, it's one biology interacting with a totally foreign biology to create a hallucination. *You are freaking hallucinating.*"

"You're wrong, Gabby."

"Sorry, dude, you're off your rocker."

"No. Listen. The compound itself acts like a computer program. 0697 is hijacking my neural pathways and controlling them like code controls transistors in a processor.

"It takes sensory input — input from a sixth sense, I think — repackages it, then sends it to my visual cortex. It adds that information to the real-world data my eyes are receiving." He grabbed my hand, "So it's not a visual hallucination. It's reinterpreted sensory input. A translation of information my brain was already receiving, but couldn't interpret. There are real lines of energy on the ground — in the ground — but that's not what I'm seeing. I'm seeing an artificial overlay, similar to a digital overlay."

I crossed my arms and raised an eyebrow skeptically. "So, there are hidden computer codes in the genes of Tums' life forms — is that what you're saying?"

"*Neural* codes."

"Right. Whatever. And what do you think you'll find at the end of this holographic rainbow? Pots o' alien gold?"

"I don't know. But, whatever it is, I think it's been waiting for us a long time."

I didn't know how to respond, so I kept my mouth shut. We didn't talk for a long time after that.

When we hit the point where the hallucination and the path parted ways, I expected Pedro to dive head-first into the wild. He didn't. He turned just as the trail did, making me wonder if his hallucination had changed. As we'd walked the sun had risen well over the horizon, which helped to ease my tensions. At least now I could see what was eating me before I dissolved into a pile of goo.

"We're getting an ATV," Pedro said out of the blue.

Ah, that explained it. He was following the path to its head: our makeshift version of a spaceport, where we stored our modest fleet of vehicles. "Good luck," I said. "With the way the base has been taken care of, I'll be surprised if anything still works at port."

Only a few minutes more saw us to our destination. The garages were sealed up much like the base, so that no one would get a nasty surprise when they opened a glove box.

As Pedro typed in the access code for one of the airlocks, I cleared my throat. "So, you know we've got two ATVs back at base, right? You didn't have to come all the way out here."

"Those are little ones. I need the big one — the wall-climber."

"The wall-climber?" I choked on my own spit. "Where exactly are we going?"

"I told you." The outer garage door opened as he gestured towards our goal.

It hadn't occurred to me that the line might go on and on and on — towards the horizon and beyond. The craggy Cizin Mountains stood directly in our path, their sheer cliffs impossible to traverse without a climber.

"But, it'll take days to get there."

"Yep."

Motion-sensing lights sprang on as we entered the hanger, and I removed my foggy helmet. The stale air indicated it had been a long time since anyone had come here. Including the maintenance guys. That didn't bode well.

The wall-climber wasn't far away. In addition to tank-tread, which most of our ATVs had, the wall-climber also sported six legs, each tipped with grasping, serrated hands. The legs were retractable, to be extended when needed.

A million protests went through my mind, but for some reason I voiced none of them. Guess I figured I was already in this, long haul or not. Why whine about it? I climbed into the ATV, lips sealed.

Inside, the vehicle was pressurized and gravity-reduced, so once we got everything up and running we could dispossess ourselves of the suits. The first thing I did, once free, was stretch out in one of the seats. Pedro blew his nose.

And then we were off. I wondered for a moment if it was smart to let the crazy man take the wheel, but I figured I didn't have much choice. Still, I double checked my harness.

Within a few hours my adrenaline ebbed, and exhaustion got the better of me. Despite my unease, I drifted off.

Luckily my instincts woke me.

Drowsy, I opened one eye and saw a needle coming at me. Acting on reflex, I swatted the syringe out of Pedro's hand. I was out of my harness and at the back of the ATV in an instant. "*What are you doing?*"

"I want you to see, too."

"That 0697 in there?" I nodded toward the syringe, now rolling freely on the floor. We were still moving — he must have had the climber on autopilot. "I took you for batty, Pedro, not dangerous."

"It's harmless," he cooed. "But it'll let you see. Give you new eyes."

"Thanks, but I'm happy with the ones madre gave me."

"You'd understand what I'm talking about it if you just took it."

"No way am I drinking your Kool-Aid, man."

He shrugged and sat back down in the driver's seat. "Fine. But I'm packaging this stuff up and sending it back to Earth. That way they can see the lines there, too."

With him safely out of range, I scooped up the syringe and dismantled it. We didn't have any bio-waste containers on board, so I made due with a rubber glove and tape from the MacGyver kit on my suit. As much as I didn't want the compound anywhere near me at this point, I didn't want to stash it where Pedro could easily get a hold of it again, either. So into my trouser pocket it went.

"What makes you think there are overlays on Earth?" I asked.

"Ley-lines. It's been long suspected that many ancients intuitively built monuments and religious centers over streams of power that cross the planet."

"Like Stonehenge?"

"Yes."

"Oh, come on. You're a scientist. How can you stomach that mumbo-jumbo, much less believe it?"

"Because there's no scientific evidence to refute their existence. And if there's no evidence that says something's impossible, I see no reason why it can't be feasible."

"How old were you when you stopped believing in Santa, huh? Twenty-five?"

"Take all the digs you want, Gabby. I know what I'm seeing is real."

Cautious, like a beaten dog, I slunk back into my seat. "Keep telling yourself that."

"I intend to."

The sun set, and rose, and set again. All the while I started to feel like a sardine: trapped in a can, nowhere to go, with only fish-tales for company. Pedro submitted to examinations when I asked him. I tested his reflexes and his reasoning skills, short term recollection and long, and looked for any sign of physical or neurological abnormality. Everything appeared in order.

I contacted the base a few times, gave them our position. I asked them about the 0697 test rats. The rodents were healthy. Slavits sent a retrieval party after us, but I doubted they'd intercept before we made it to the bottom of the cliffs.

And I was right. The sun rose, glazing the range from top to bottom in brilliant, orange light. The jungle-line ended a mile or so before the cliffs, leaving a barren mote between the two. I gulped as we entered into it, feeling exposed.

My backup was still hours away.

"Relax, Gabby," Pedro said as he prepared to extend the climber's arms. "I've trained in this thing. We'll be safe."

But the climb wasn't what worried me. "And what if we get to the top of the mountains and the line keeps going, huh? Miles and miles and miles — how far are we going? How many ration packets does this thing have stored? Enough for a week, two maybe? The water's already running low."

"We won't be gone that long. I see where it ends." He pointed up.

I ducked down lower, peering through the windshield as though I could see what he saw. "In the side of the cliff?"

"Yep."

"Oh boy."

He pressed a few buttons and the cabin filled with an ear-piercing screech.

"Gah." I threw my hands over my ears. "What the hell was that?" The sounds of stressed metal reverberated through the cabin.

"One of the arms is stuck." Lights flashed across the console. "I'm trying the overrides, but nothing's working. It must be an outside problem. Might have to fix it manually."

My suit and helmet were in hand the next moment. "Ok, just show me what to do."

Once suited, we exited through the rear airlock. Pedro went first. "Just over here — it's limb three."

"Hey," I said, turning back. I saw a spray canister sitting against the hyper-glass. "You forgot your tranquilizer. Gotta stun the wildlife." I went in after it.

"Relax," he said. "We're a ways from the bush-line. Not many animals venture out from the brush."

Sprayer in hand, I swung around to join him. "Yeah, well you never—"

"*Ghraaaaa!*"

His scream was unearthly. The bottom dropped out of my stomach and my nerves caught fire. I must have jumped ten feet in the air, despite the high grav. When I came back down I was sure I'd separated my skin from my bones in the leap.

Pedro lay sprawled across the ground, shaking. I slid through the dirt into a crouch by his side. It only took me moments to put together the scene: Pedro hemorrhaging, a massive pool of blood coalescing where his right knee should have continued on into calf; his severed leg bouncing along the ground towards the bush-line; a long, silvery cord of carnivorous guillotine vine attached to the leg, slithering back from whence it came.

Blood loss and decompression. Code red. A top priority medical emergency, and all I had to deal with it was whatever first-aid supplies the ATV had stocked.

Hands shaking, I dug through my MacGyver kit, looking for tourniquet material. All I had was a short piece of cord and a handkerchief. Better than nothing.

My breath came in quick, heavy puffs against the inside of my helmet. It fogged up the corner, making a dire job much more difficult. Adrenaline, which had surged at his first yelp, left me unsteady. Every part of my body vibrated.

I hadn't stopped the bleeding, but the flow was slower. The most devastating aspect of a guillotine vine was its smooth cut — no ragged edges or pinched flesh to staunch the bleeding. Pedro's artery had been cut clean open, letting it run like an open faucet.

If there wasn't any coagulant cement in the ATV, he'd be dead in minutes.

The suit's skeleton finally paid for itself. Instead of dragging Pedro, I was able to lift him fully off the ground. I tossed him through the airlock, knowing every second I wasted screwed him over a little more.

Yanking the emergency kit off the wall, I began yelling at him. It was the best outlet for my energy. Took the shakes out of my fingers. "You *son of a bitch*." I tore the lid form the kit and dumped it on the floor. Small bottles rolled this way and that. I snatched up one after the other, glancing at the labels before tossing the useless ones aside.

"You *ass*. You crazy ass. Why'd I think for a second you'd use an ounce of caution? No, crazy, stupid, ass-wipe Pedro had to go and tangle with a stupid vine. Dumb way to go, amigo. That what you want your tombstone to read? Killed by a vegetable? Idiot. Where's your brain, huh?"

Found it — the cement. Thank the lord. I had a glop of it on my glove in the next instant and smeared the stuff all over his leaking wound.

"Shooting yourself up with experimental drugs, going outside without so much as a flashlight, strolling across an alien surface like you own the place. Dumbass. Everything here wants to eat you. There's no holy-alien-grail out there waiting for you. Just some crazy shit messing with your senses." I found a pressure cuff and secured it around the stump, putting a temporary seal on his damaged suit.

He hadn't made a sound since his scream. Not so much as a moan. And now he lay perfectly still. I couldn't see his face inside his helmet, and mine was getting blurry —

It wasn't until a tear splashed down and collected in the low point of my helmet that I realized I was crying.

A squeeze on my glove made me jump. "Keep going," Pedro breathed.

"You selfish, low-life, scum-sucking—"

He let out a wheezy laugh. "No. Up. Keep going. Follow the lines."

My mouth flopped open. "Hell no." I got to my feet, simultaneously throwing off my streaky helmet. "We are turning this sucker around. We're intercepting backup and hoping they have a skimmer that can buzz you to base before you croak."

A moment of panic overtook me, and I rushed to the driver's seat. We were going back, *now*. Pedro could shove his ridiculous quest. I wasn't going to sit out here and let him die for psudo-science.

The engine purred and the warning lights still flashed impatiently. "Yeah, yeah. I'll get to you," I said, waving the urgent alerts aside, then opening a comm. channel to the intercept team. "Hey, where are you guys? We've got a medical emergency. Alvarez is—" A steamy *hiss* and an all-too familiar *thud* interrupted me. "Oh, please…" I moaned. My forehead had a brief date with the dash before I turned to look at the back of the ATV.

Members of the backup team chattered over the comm., but I didn't comprehend a word. My ears had tuned out. The totality of my awareness was focused on Pedro.

He sat in the airlock, separated from me by one set of hyper-glass doors, and Tums' surface by another.

"What in the…" I reached for my helmet, but it was gone. He had it with him in the airlock. Not a good sign. I found his suit's channel with the ATV's comm-link. "Buddy? Whatcha doin'?"

A half laugh, half cough preceded his explanation. "Blackmailing you."

"How's that?"

"We're not going back, Gabby. Not without reaching the end. If you don't keep going, I'll let myself out." He reached up and tapped the control panel.

Dude had lost too much blood and wasn't thinking straight. Rolling my eyes, I pressed the main release for the inner doors. No need to stretch this charade out.

Nothing happened. So I pressed again, and again, each time with a little more malice. "What did you do, Pedro?"

"Triggered the emergency override."

"You can only do that if the main cabin is in danger of decompress—" It took half a second for me to jump out of the driver's seat and cross the distance to the glass. "Pedro, so help me…"

"The vine was up inside the suspension, probably further — didn't you see its spent acid pods?" He patted the wall. "No holes in the system yet, or we'd be hearing sirens, but there's a weak spot somewhere. We're both in danger. Keep going and I'll come inside and give you your helmet back. Refuse and I'll go out there."

"You are ridiculous," I spat. "You see all this blood on the floor? It's supposed to be in your brain. That's what's keeping you from thinking right. You might just be demented enough to die for your cause, but there's no way you're a murderer. Now stop playing, we need to get you to the medlab." Pedro wasn't a killer. He had to be bluffing.

"I can't stop now. I might die anyway. I'd rather die knowing." He looked paler than moments before, and sweat soaked his brow line.

If he fainted on me that would be the end of us, bluff or no. "Ok," I said, pressing my palms to the glass. "We'll go." Like hell. As soon as he blacked out we were on our way to base.

"Forgive me for not trusting you, Gabby, but that's not going to convince me. There's only one way I'll come out of here." Each word was separated by a strained pause.

"What? Tell me."

"You have to take 0697."

Unbelievable. "Did I do something bad to you in a past life?"

"Stop your moaning and do it."

There wasn't time for a rundown of the pros and cons. "This is nuts, this is nuts, this is nuts," I chanted, freeing myself from the top-half of my suit so I could reach my trouser pocket and the vile vial inside.

The first-aid kit had a packet of clean needles. I tore one open with my teeth, untaped the glove and the plunger, and put the syringe containing 0697 back together.

After a series of deep breaths, I held out my forearm and poised the needle like a practiced drug addict. Only, unlike an addict, I hesitated.

What the hell was I doing? We still didn't know the full effects of the compound. I was less sure now — after all the tests — that it fried brain cells, but that didn't mean it was safe. What if we got Pedro back, sealed his leg up, but he still died? From side effects?

What if it killed me too?

But, if I didn't inject myself we were goners anyway. Better possible death than certain.

Pedro watched me with dilated pupils. His skin looked like soggy paper.

"Hope this makes you happy, bud." With that I thrust the needle into my arm and pushed the plunger in to its hilt. Job complete, I tossed the dirty needle aside. "Now open up!"

He keyed in the access code, fingers shaking like leaves in the wind. The door opened and he slumped over, letting himself rest, sure now that his epic task would be completed.

Since he was out like a light and limp as a sack of beans, I had to pull him across the floor and strap him in the passenger seat. "If this crap poisons me, I'll kill you," I promised, hyped up and running through the gambit of emotions. One second I wanted to weep, and the next I wanted to wring his neck.

How long was it supposed to take before the effects showed up? With my heart racing a million miles a minute, pushing my blood through my veins at an alarming pace, I guessed it wouldn't be long.

We needed to get to the tracking party asap. I sat my butt down in the driver's seat, secured my helmet, then threw the ATV into reverse. The warning lights still signaled the cabin was in danger of losing its integrity, but at least the arms were free (I'm guessing the vine had tried to chop the limb off for breakfast before it pegged Pedro for squishier). I radioed back to base, told them to prepare the medlab for two patients.

Minutes later I was attempting to blink neon-yellow streamers from my eyes. They appeared on the floor — *through* the floor. The images started out hazy and spotty, but soon solidified. Looking up I could see an entire system, all the way to the next horizon, back the direction we'd come as well as stretched out ahead. It was a giant, mapped overlay. Pulsing, flowing, like little pieces of light shifting to form streaming messages I could not read.

Startled, I hit the brakes.

Damn. He was right. Pedro was right. There *was* something hidden in the biology of Cit-Bolon-Tum.

Or, now we were both crazy. Folie a deux. But, what were the odds of a shared hallucination, really?

And then I felt the pull. An alarming, palpable urge to follow the lines. It was the current Pedro had talked about — a rushing, pushing me forward. First it was like the gentle thrust of a stream, but soon it consumed me like a riptide. I had to go forward, had to see what was at the end of the road.

A moan escaped Pedro, and I turned to see if he'd come around. He was still unconscious, but alive.

Poor Pedro. What must it be like, to believe so heartily in possibilities that you'd risk your life for a chance at proof? To be so free of cynicism as to follow leads with reckless abandonment?

It was stupid, but it was also beautifully human. And an experience I'd never had.

Everyone should do something truly idiotic at least once in their life, right?

I knew I needed to get us back to base. We both needed medical attention. But I also knew I had to follow the lines — and it wasn't just the compound talking.

Abandoning my suspicion and sarcasm, I took a leap of faith. "We're gonna make it," I said, giving Pedro a pat on the arm. "We're gonna find out what's at the end of your rainbow."

I spun the ATV around and quickly covered the distance to the cliff face. At the base I extended the legs, shifted into high gear, and started to climb.

I'd only driven the climber once before — in training. This was nothing like the exercises. Every new anchor and handhold sent a little thrill of anxiety up my spine.

Good thing I was in a chemically induced mania, or else there's no way I would have continued up that cliff.

I tried to keep my eyes on both the climb and Pedro's condition, and glanced rapidly between the two. "Don't die on me, buddy."

It's so much easier to follow a map when you can actually see it. The lines didn't continue straight as they had before. Now they slanted at a forty-five, and ahead I could see it change course again. Another fifteen minutes and I pinpointed our destination: a narrow-mouthed cave. Two yellow streamers poured into it, one from above, and the one I followed from below.

Halfway there the climber grabbed onto a loose boulder. It pulled free, and the weight of the stone dragged the arm down. The whole vehicle slipped. I tried not to scream, for Pedro's sake.

Rocks flew past the windows, plummeting towards the ground. I couldn't help but imagine our frail bodies doing the same.

Regaining my poise, I pushed on. We reached the cavern without another hitch, and I thanked my lucky stars it would all be over soon.

I positioned the climber above the cavern so that I could open the rear airlock and lower myself inside. Before I left I secured Pedro, double checked my suit, and made sure I had a sprayer. The bay doors screeched open, and I realized I hadn't tied down everything. The spent syringe and a few items from the first-aid kit tumbled through the airlock. I let them go.

There was no lip to the cave. It recessed straight back into the rock, its mouth flush with the cliff. I tied a cable to the back of the vehicle, and, holding my breath, slowly slid down its length.

People say it's not a good idea to look down when you're stranded at a great height. What a load of crap. Nothing solidifies your determination not to fall like knowing how far it is to the ground.

The ATV sat close to the cave — I'd parked like an expert. Putting a little swing in the cable, I propelled myself inside.

Hundreds of glowing, beady eyes turned my way the instant I touched down. Only my knowledge of the drop-off kept me from darting right back outside again.

Shit. Damn. Crap. I didn't have enough tranquilizer for a cave full of critters.

But I steadied myself and moved forwards. Most of the eyes hovered around the ceiling — the floor was left clear. I didn't dare turn on my light, fearing they'd go into a frenzy and attack.

Just let me get to the back of the cave. Let me see what's in here and I'll never bother you again, I silently pleaded with them.

The lines still pointed the way. One thick, center line shifted the most — it was the one that looked like it contained a message. Its color suddenly changed, now bright pink.

I could no longer see the eyes, and the suit kept me from hearing any noise the animals might have made. My entire body clenched — every joint stiffened. It was my worst nightmare come true — trapped in a cave with vermin. Vermin that could leap out of the darkness and start chewing at any minute. Chew through my suit, my clothes, my skin, my bones…

I almost ran. I almost said, *screw it.*

But the program in my brain wouldn't let me. My overwhelming urge to *discover* continued to propel me forward.

And there was that something else — something that drove me besides the compound. Loyalty to Pedro, perhaps?

The cave turned out to be shallow. I'd anticipated a deep, winding system, but only a few yards in I reached its rear. Here the lines wound up the wall, abandoning their angularity, curling around what appeared to be a vault door.

Superimposed symbols glowed over its center, and beneath the holographic designs were real-world counterparts. The overlay continuously changed, revealing a pattern. Instructions, I realized

— a key code. All I had to do was touch the designs in the indicated order.

Done. The door unlocked. Vapor poured out from the seams, similar to the way it seeped from newly opened cryo-tubes.

A cold shiver shook my body. An image of a small, frozen alien intelligence — rat-like, tail, whiskers and all — came into my mind.

Be damned if I was going to touch anything like that. Pedro could wake the hell up and come get it himself.

But no rat-men were revealed when the door swung outwards. Instead the vault contained a massive store of mug-sized vials. Containers in row after row, thousands of them, stretching back into the rock — all sealed in a way that was unfamiliar to me. Fuchsia liquid, frigid but not frozen, sat inside each vial.

The overlay turned green and produced another pattern — it showed me how to open the containers.

And words — the same unreadable words as in the ley-line — ran across the outside like a label. Bizarrely, I knew what the liquid was for. No question in my mind.

I grabbed one and ran, slamming the door behind me.

The percussion must have startled the cave inhabitants, because they went wild.

Dark forms fell from the ceiling, onto the floor and onto *me*. I called out, batting them away, bee-lining for the entrance. The sprayer was little help. It created a cloud of tranquilizer that only succeeded in making more animals fall from the ceiling.

The damn cave was raining rodents.

Someone in the universe was having a laugh at my expense, I was sure.

I dropped the sprayer and leapt for the cable, using only one hand to grab it since I'd tucked the vial under my arm football-style. The suit-skeleton won again, giving my arm and legs the added strength they needed to haul me back into the climber.

With the airlock and the bay doors tightly shut behind me, I began shedding the unconscious tag-alongs. They were as hideous as I feared. Amorphous, multi-eyeballed, hairy blobs with frightening incisors. To my knowledge, an undocumented species. I'd toss them out the airlock as soon as I'd taken care of the real business at hand — someone else could come back for a specimen.

I pulled Pedro's helmet off and followed the alien instructions to a T. The vial opened, revealing its viscous insides. Without skipping a beat, I poured the whole thing down his throat.

Exhausted, I let the empty container fall to the floor and roll back towards the airlock. I carefully replaced his helmet, and seconds later the decompression sirens finally sounded — the weak spot had given in. Perfect timing. I assured the ATV that all passengers were suited, and it stopped yelling. Then I took up the driver's seat once again, knowing I couldn't rest until we'd made it back home.

A week later Pedro was still in the recovery wing — but his leg was growing back nicely.

"We came here looking for medical answers," I said to him, holding up the empty vial. "I just wasn't expecting to find them like this."

"I told you," he said with a smile.

"No, you told me about an alien road-map. Not an alien regenerative serum."

He took the container from me and turned it over in his hands. "You know, I think each planet has a purpose. A piece of a greater puzzle. We figure it out, and we get the rewards. They set up a planet with great medicinal prospects so we'd come here with a purpose.

We were clever enough to find the map — even if it was on accident — so we got the medicine."

"Sounds a little like rats in a maze," I said, "Get to the center and you find the cheese."

Pedro shrugged and sat back against his pillow. "Maybe it is. I thought the ley-lines pointed to a greater intelligence waiting for us to evolve, to become intelligent enough to interact with them. You know, like equals. But maybe you're right. Maybe we're just lab rats. An experiment."

"Either way, you did it. You discovered proof of—" I still wanted to gag on the word, "— *Seeding*. By a greater intelligence."

He nodded, but didn't smile. "Bet there are more caves out there, filled with this stuff."

"We'll just have to keep following the overlays," I said. "Which has me thinking."

Pedro looked me in the eye, curious. "What?"

"Well, this planet had a distinct purpose with a distinct prize. If all ley-lines are real… what do you think Earth's lines point to?"

He raised an eyebrow and we shared a long look. "Don't know," he said eventually, "But I'd give my other leg to find out."

Marina J. Lostetter and her husband, Alex, live in Northwest Arkansas with two Tasmanian devils--no, wait, those are house cats. Marina's original short fiction has appeared in venues such as *Lightspeed*, *InterGalactic Medicine Show*, and *Shimmer Magazine*, and her debut novel, *Noumenon* is available from Harper Voyager.

She tweets as @MarinaLostetter, and her website can be found at www.lostetter.net.

FUEL

First published in Cosmos Online (April 2009)

Matthew S. Rotundo

The third quarter report cards came out Thursday, and for Jamie, the timing couldn't have been worse. The Nike man was coming over that night to sell his brother some new blood.

He took his time walking home from Gilder Middle School, weaving past cracks in the sidewalk and mud puddles left behind by the spring thaw. His pace slowed further as he turned onto Willow Avenue and saw his house, second on the left, a red brick ranch with spidery ivy growing up the east side. Old leaves, fallen tree branches, and other detritus left over from the winter littered the front yard. As he neared, he noted with dismay his father's car already in the driveway.

"Damn." Jamie trudged across the yard and let himself in the front door with his keycard.

Dad was at the hall closet, hanging up his overcoat. He stood just under two meters tall; a navy blue business suit wrapped his muscled frame. He beamed when he saw Jamie. "Hey there, kiddo. How was school today?"

"You're home early," Jamie said.

"Need to get ready for the presentation tonight. And I'd like you to clean up the front yard. Make sure you use the dirt rake to get up that thatch. Will you do that for me?"

Jamie opened his mouth to protest, but thought the better of it. "Sure," he said. He unslung his backpack and headed for the stairs.

"Oh. By the way." Dad fished in a suit pocket and produced a folded piece of paper. "I got this in my email today." He opened the paper.

Jaime recognized the school's letterhead on the printout. He slumped, leaning against the wall.

Dad tapped the paper. "What's this C-plus in Basic Fitness about, kiddo?"

"I got A's in my academic classes. They're all honors courses, too."

"I can see that. But we've talked about Fitness before, haven't we?" Dad looked down at him with a disapproving arch of an eyebrow.

"Yes."

"So tell me. What happened?"

"It's nothing. I'll do better next quarter."

"Did you fail the agility drills again?"

"I couldn't do the pull-ups."

Dad pressed his lips together and took a breath. "I'm not sure you're giving it your best effort, Jamie."

"I am. I really am. I'm just not very good at sports."

"You get better with practice. Like your brother Scott."

Jamie nodded, keeping his gaze down, hoping Dad didn't notice the way he gritted his teeth when he heard his older brother's name.

Dad clapped him on the shoulder. "Jamie, you're twelve years old now. It's really important that you find your best sport. College recruiters are already contacting boys your age."

Jamie thought of his best friend Russell, who had just gotten his first recruiting letter the other day, from Penn State. Jamie hung his head even lower.

"All I'm asking is that you try, son. Will you do that for me?"

Jamie nodded again.

Dad folded up the grade printout and stuffed it into a pocket. "Hey, I have an idea. Why don't you sit in on the presentation tonight?"

"Oh, man." Jamie looked up. "Do I have to, Dad?"

"Why not? Maybe you'll hear something you like."

A groan escaped Jamie. He had homework to do for Advanced Literature — the next two chapters of *Dracula*, which he'd loved so far. But experience had taught him not to proffer academic work as an excuse. "Why don't you guys just order Scott's blood online? That's what you usually do."

"The Nike representative wants to show us some new and improved stuff. The best yet. Scott has regionals in two weeks, you know."

"I know."

"So. You'll be there tonight, then?"

"Sure, Dad."

Dad clapped him on the shoulder again. "That's the spirit. Now let's get that yard picked up, OK?"

Jamie went upstairs to change out of his school clothes before getting to work.

"Fuel 6.1 is our latest release, and our best," the Nike man said. "You can see from the charts how our refined erythrocyte design maximizes oxygen-carbon dioxide exchange, nutrient absorption, and hormone capacity. You folks have probably read about all that stuff already; it was part of the 6.0 rollout. But 6.1 also features enhanced thrombocyte function that increases fibrinogen production by as much as fifty percent. It lasts longer than 6.0, too. You can go up to four weeks without a new transfusion. And of course, Fuel still has the highest-quality, FDA-approved leukocytes and plasma substitutes available on the market."

The Nike man topped two meters, taller than even Dad. He had dark hair streaked blonde. His skin was so deeply tanned that Jamie could swear it glowed. The salesman's hands seemed huge, each big enough on its own to comfortably grip a basketball. He wore an immaculate black workout singlesuit that flowed with his movements. And he had the shoes, of course. Top of the line SuperJumps, solid black, like the suit.

He made his pitch in the living room, with the aid of handouts and multimedia charts from a display that stood on its own tripod. Mom and Dad, seated on the couch, paid close attention, nodding at appropriate times, asking occasional questions, laughing at the salesman's jokes. Scott, just turned sixteen, long-legged and lanky, slumped between them with his arms crossed. His gaze wandered as the Nike man talked. Jamie sat in the rocking chair to one side, next to the bookcase filled with Scott's track trophies and medals.

The Nike man continued: "Athletes using Fuel 6.1 have shown documented increases in metabolism, endurance, and recovery from injury. And if you purchase tonight, we'll even throw in a free home transfusion kit."

Jamie shook his head. Scott already had one of those. Jamie had set it up for him many times, usually on nights before track meets. Jamie had grown more proficient working the kit than his parents.

He glanced at the clock on the wall. The time was just after seven o'clock. If the Nike man finished his spiel in the next hour, Jamie would still be able to do some of his Advanced Lit homework.

"Wow," Dad said, smiling and nodding. "That's something, isn't it, Scott?"

"I guess," Scott said.

The Nike man gave an amused smile. "You don't sound convinced."

"I'm a sprinter. I don't care about all that endurance stuff."

"What's your forty time, Scott?"

"Four-one-five."

"Not bad. But suppose I were to tell you that Fuel 6.1 can improve your personal best by as much as a full second?"

"Yeah, right," Scott said. "Whatever."

"Regionals are only two weeks away, honey," Mom said. She was small and wiry, with closely cropped hair and an angular face. She still wore work clothes — white top, pinstriped jacket and skirt, heels. "And didn't your coach say you need to get under four seconds if you want to—"

Scott cut her off with an exasperated sigh and a roll of his eyes. An awkward silence fell.

The Nike man turned toward Jamie in the rocking chair. "How about you, Jimmy? This stuff is pretty cool, huh?"

"Uh…it's *Jamie*."

The Nike man put on a let's-be-friends smile. "Do you think you would like to try Fuel? I'll bet you'd like it."

The salesman's radiant good health made Jamie uncomfortably conscious of the paunch around his middle. "Um…no, thanks."

"Why not? This is quality stuff, you know."

With a sidelong glance toward his parents, Jamie said, "That's OK."

The Nike man's smile became indulgent. "I understand, Jamie. You think that you could never be an athlete like your brother, or all the other kids. But 6.1 could be the key for you. Blood *is* just like fuel, you know. The better the fuel, the better your body will work. In no time at all, you could be running track like your brother—"

Scott laughed. Mom shushed him.

" — or, with your size, maybe playing football. I could see you fitting in well at guard, or possibly even center."

"You know, that's what I keep telling him," Dad said.

Jamie's cheeks burned. Why couldn't the guy just leave him alone and get on with the presentation?

The Nike man said, "You really shouldn't overlook the benefits of athletic competition. Athletes are much less likely to get involved with drugs or alcohol, or drop out of school. You might even get to attend college on an athletic scholarship, if you're good enough."

"Will it make me smarter?"

Dad cleared his throat.

The Nike man cast a puzzled glance toward the couch. "Well...Fuel is designed to enhance *athletic* performance."

"He's taking all *academic* classes," Scott said with a sneer.

"I see." The Nike man's smile thinned.

"He's still taking Basic Fitness. And he hasn't even started his Nutrition courses. Hell, when I was Jamie's age, I had already gone through Advanced Conditioning."

"We're, ah, we're very proud of him." Mom, glancing uneasily at Jamie, patted Scott's knee.

"I'll bet."

Jamie glowered at his smirking brother. "I got A's in all my honors courses this quarter."

The Nike man said, "Jamie, academic scholarships are mighty hard to come by these days. Take it from me, most schools just don't have the necessary funding."

Jamie looked at the floor. In a mumble, he said, "I guess I don't care."

"I'm sorry, Jamie; I missed that. What did you say?"

Jamie's mouth drew tight, like a drawstring bag. The collective stare of his parents, his brother, and the Nike man weighed on him, suffusing him with a deep weariness.

"Jamie? What did you say?"

He raised his chin, scowling. "I said, *I don't care.* All right? You happy now?"

The Nike man took a step backward.

"I don't like football. Get it? I don't like track, either. I don't like sports. I got A's in all my honors courses. Now will you just leave me alone? Please?"

His heart raced. He breathed heavily, as if he'd just run around the block. He wondered at his own words. Had he actually just spoken them in front of his parents? He turned to the couch, suddenly terrified.

"Jee-*zus*." Scott stood suddenly. "Do I have to stay down here and listen to this crap, Dad? You've already ordered my blood. This guy's just here to talk to Jamie, anyway."

"Scott, you be *quiet*!" Mom glared at him.

"Why? It's true, isn't it? You're just trying to get him with the program. Waste of time, if you ask me. His buddy's already getting scholarship offers, and fat little Jamie just hides in his books. He's a friggin' loser."

Dad stood, too. His face was stern. "That's enough out of you, young man. You may go to your room."

Scott set hands on hips. "And what if I don't? You gonna ground me? I have regionals in two weeks. You wouldn't want me to miss practice, would you?"

Mom and Dad exchanged glances. The Nike man looked at his perfect shoes.

"Shit. I'm going over to Kevin's." Scott stormed out the front door, slamming it hard enough to rattle the windows. One of Mom's ceramic angel figurines fell from the knickknack shelf. The carpet cushioned its fall.

Jamie gaped at his parents. Neither one would meet his gaze.

And he understood why the Nike man was here. Why his parents hadn't just ordered the new blood online, as they usually did. Why Dad had insisted on Jamie being present for the presentation. Why the Nike man had focused so much attention on him.

Jamie looked around the room. His gaze found the multimedia display on its tripod, charting the performance-enhancing benefits of Fuel. He had never felt so alone in all his life.

Slowly, he got to his feet. His throat double-clutched. "I think...I'm gonna be sick." He headed for the bathroom on unsteady legs.

The sun had long since set before a timid knock came at Jamie's bedroom door. It opened, and Mom entered. In the darkness, she was only a silhouette.

"Jamie? Are you awake?"

He lay supine on his bed. "Yeah."

She sat on the edge of the bed. "Honey, I'm so sorry about what happened tonight."

"It's okay, Mom. I'm sorry, too. For what I said."

"Your father and I just don't want you to miss out on any opportunities. Your friend Russell—"

"I've been thinking, Mom. I'd like to try the new blood."

"You would?" She put a hand on his arm. "Oh, Jamie, are you sure?"

"I'm sure. Can we still get the free transfusion kit?"

"Well, actually...we hoped you would change your mind. We ordered the blood for you. The kit's downstairs."

"Oh. Good. Is it very much different from Scott's?"

"Looks the same, I think. You should be able to assemble it yourself. You'll probably be able to do your own transfusions, even." She leaned over and kissed his forehead. "You're growing up. Your father and I are very proud of you."

Jamie was grateful for the darkness, so that his mother could not see his face twist with pain.

"You get some sleep now," Mom said. She stood and looked down at him for a moment. Jamie imagined that she was probably smiling. Then she left, quietly shutting the door behind her.

Tears threatened, but Jamie fought them down. He had much too much to think about.

After his first transfusion, he would have a whole body's worth of blood left over. *Normal* blood. Usually, it was sent to the Nike people for recycling. But if Jamie could somehow hide it instead — store it in the basement freezer, maybe — then...

Regionals were only two weeks away. Scott would do a fresh transfusion the night before; he always did. Jamie would help him with it, as usual. And he and Scott had the same blood type.

In the darkness, Jamie smiled. The Nike man had called it Fuel. Well, knowledge was a kind of fuel, too. Mom and Dad and Scott didn't understand that. Not yet, anyway.

He would get in serious trouble, of course. But it would be worth the punishment if, only for a moment, they would understand him at last. It would ease the loneliness.

Still smiling, Jamie drifted off to sleep.

Matthew S. Rotundo wrote his first story—"The Elephant and the Cheese"—when he was eight years old. It was the first time he had ever filled an entire page with writing. To his young mind, that seemed like a major accomplishment. It occurred to him shortly thereafter that writing stories was what he wanted to do with his life.

In addition to Writers of the Future, Matt has attended the prestigious Odyssey Writer's workshop and won the Science Fiction Writers of Earth Contest and Phobos Award.

More at www.matthewsrotundo.com.

Miss Davenport's Ugly Cat

First published in Cats In Space (May 2015)

C. L. Holland

The thing that came out of the box wasn't a cat, it was an alien. It had the markings of one of those black-and-whites they call tuxedos, but it was completely hairless, with baggy skin like it was wearing a suit several sizes too big.

"This is George," Miss Davenport said.

I turned to the captain. "I thought you said it was a cat."

"It *is* a cat, Munroe," he replied. "Even if it is a damn ugly one." Miss Davenport tutted and without breaking stride he added, "Beg your pardon ma'am, but you've got to admit he's unusual-looking."

"He's a Sphynx," Miss Davenport said. "They're bred to look like that. I'd have thought a well-travelled man such as yourself would have known, Captain."

"I'm not an animal person, ma'am." He gestured at me. "Get him back in the box. Miss Davenport will arrange for his things to be delivered to your quarters." The cat stared at me with its flat yellow eyes. My skin crawled at the thought of touching anything so scrotally grotesque, but luckily Miss Davenport scooped him up.

The cat batted at her half-heartedly. I turned my attention to the other thing that bothered me.

"My quarters, sir?"

"Where else would you keep him? It's only until we reach the next spaceport."

"Then why can't Miss Davenport keep him? Sir." The captain sighed, and pinched the bridge of his nose. "Because she shouldn't have a cat on a liner at all. If I let her keep him it may encourage our other senior residents to bring unauthorised animals on board."

"Oh, some of them already have," Miss Davenport interrupted. "That's why Hetty reported poor George - it was Hetty, wasn't it Captain? She thinks he'll eat her mice."

The captain stared at her. "Look into it, Munroe, we can't have mice on the ship. And get that cat out of here."

"Yes, sir."

Miss Davenport put George back in his box and handed it to me. In the corridor she patted my hand.

"Don't be put off by how he looks, dear. George is a big old softy really."

"Good to know." It wasn't like I planned to hug the creature. Four days to the Lansdowne Eight, the next port, and I could hand it off to an animal sanctuary.

"If he's any trouble, give me a call," she said. "I'm not going anywhere." She was only half joking. Miss Davenport was one of what our captain called "senior residents" and the rest of us called "lifers". In the twentieth century it was popular among older people who could afford it to live in hotels. They'd pack everything they needed into a couple of rooms, eat in the restaurant, and housekeeping would clean their bathroom and change their sheets. Now, those who could afford it lived on intergalactic cruise liners instead. It was like living in a hotel, only you got to see the universe and the entertainment was better. There were a good dozen or so lifers on the QE11 alone.

Back in my quarters, I deposited the box on my coffee table and regarded the dark shape inside. George stared back at me, unblinking.

"What am I going to do with you? I can't give you the run of the place." I wondered if there was an empty crate down in the hold, that I could turn into a makeshift run. Although space would be a problem in my quarters, and the hold was temperature regulated to Unpleasantly Cool. Didn't cats like it warm?

"You can go in the bathroom," I said, wondering that I was already talking to the cat like I thought it would answer me. I took the box into, well, a bigger box. The bathroom was only big enough for a toilet and a shower cubicle, but it would give the cat some space to roam while I figured out what to do with it.

I put the box on the lid of the toilet, slipped the catch, and shut the door behind me as I left.

Hetty - that is, Mrs Fletcher - went pale when she opened the door and saw me there in my orange overalls. Where Miss Davenport was tall and thin, she was small and stocky. Her hair, more grey than white, was cut short.

"Mr Munroe," she said. "What a lovely surprise. Do come in. Can I offer you some tea?"

"No thank you, Mrs Fletcher." I glanced around her sitting room, which was bigger than my whole cabin, but couldn't see any sign of animal inhabitants that weren't made of china. "I've had a report of unauthorised animals on the premises."

She sighed theatrically. "Well you would, wouldn't you. After I reported Josie's monstrosity she was bound to report my little darlings." It took me a moment to realise she meant Miss Davenport and George. "Only I didn't think it was safe. Cats like to roam. What if he got in the tubes or the engine? He could space us all. Cats like to chew things. And do their business where they shouldn't."

"So do mice, Mrs Fletcher."

She sagged into her purple jumper. "I suppose they do. It's just pleasant to have another life around, being so far from home."

"Will you turn them over to me?"

"I would if I still had them. They escaped." She looked sheepish.

There were mice loose on the ship. They could be anywhere, finding all the tiny holes and chewable things. This was worse than an elderly resident with an ugly cat.

Mrs Fletcher showed me where she'd kept them. The cage was still full of shredded paper and mouse droppings.

"I must have left the cage door open," Mrs Fletcher said.

"How did you hide them from housekeeping?"

"I hid the cage in my wardrobe. I didn't mean any harm, Mr Munroe."

I bit back my first reaction - that this would be a great comfort if they destroyed, say, the life support systems. "I'm sure you didn't."

Mrs Fletcher let me conduct a brief inspection of her cabin, to make sure the mice really had disappeared. There was no sign of them, and I could only assume they'd disappeared into the ventilation system, or escaped out the door when it was opened.

When I got back to my cabin, George blinked at me sleepily from the couch. The bathroom door stood open. For a moment I wondered if I'd forgotten to shut it, but the look of satisfaction on the cat's face suggested otherwise. His radar-dish ears swivelled and a moment later the door buzzer went.

Miss Davenport waited outside, laden down with bags and a huge plastic box. I'd seen parents with toddlers carrying fewer accessories.

"You didn't have to bring all that yourself, ma'am."

"I know. I've never had an excuse to visit crew quarters before. I'm nosy like that." She handed me the box and followed me in. "Terribly small, isn't it? You don't have any windows?"

"The portholes are reserved for paying customers, ma'am."

"It's probably for the best. While the view is spectacular, there's something about a permanent night sky that makes it difficult to get out of bed in the morning."

We unpacked the bags and boxes onto the counter. There were two types of food, a litter tray, cat litter, toys, a bed, and a selection of little knitted jackets in pastel colours. I picked up a pink one.

"You made this?"

"Heavens no, my sister did. George was her cat, I just inherited him. I can't say I was terribly pleased, George and I have never more than tolerated each other. But I promised I'd find him a home with someone better suited to his temperament. I owe my sister that much. Well, I did my best."

I tried to lighten the mood. "At least being hairless he won't need much grooming."

"Oh no dear, he needs plenty. A peculiarity of the breed. Bathtime once a week, he's due one before we reach port. Here's his shampoo." Miss Davenport handed me a bottle of milky pink liquid. "He's quite good with water, so don't let him tell you he isn't." I glanced sideways at George, who paused in licking his privates to stare back blankly.

"He feels the cold quite keenly, so keep him warm. That's what the jackets are for, although I'm sure he dislikes them as much as I do. Cats have a very strong sense of dignity, they know when they look stupid."

If I hadn't seen her sister's knitted creations, I'd have thought it difficult for George to look any sillier.

"What do I do if he gets out?" If he could open the bathroom, he could probably get out of the cabin.

"He probably won't, but a good rattle of his biscuits will usually bring him running. The greedy little creature can't get enough of them."

As if just the mention of biscuits was enough to summon him, George hopped up on the counter to investigate. He purred as he rubbed his face against the boxes and bags. Then he hopped into the box and his purr gained a bass echo as he settled.

"He also loves boxes," Miss Davenport said. "Well, I'll leave you two to get acquainted. Let me know when you're free when we get to port, and I'll help you find a home for him."

"You're not sad to see him go?"

"I'm sure things will work out for the best, dear. These things always do."

I set up George's litter tray alongside the toilet and put the rest of his things back into the bags. George and his box went in a corner. He jumped out immediately, so I dropped his bed in the box and hoped he'd take the hint.

He didn't. As soon as I sat down, he climbed up on the sofa beside me. He pushed his face into mine and rubbed up against my hand as I pushed him away. His skin was so warm I could see why he'd be sensitive to the cold, and softer than I expected.

"Settle down, you daft creature."

He settled, flopping down on his side with a look of contentment.

Ten minutes later, when he was asleep with his paws wrapped around my forearm, I didn't have the heart to wake him.

"Hear you've got a cat, Chief," Mac, my second in command, greeted me at the engine room. "Never would have figured you for an animal person."

"It's only until we reach port." I explained what had happened, and I could see him trying not to laugh. "Nice to know you care."

"It might solve our other problem, actually. Mrs Fletcher's mice."

"We can't let a cat loose in the conduits, anything could happen. We'd lose him too." Even rattling a box of biscuits probably wouldn't bring him back, and I owed it to Miss Davenport to see George safely to his new home.

Mac shrugged. "Just a thought."

The mice probably wouldn't breed before we reached port, but they could do a hell of a lot of damage.

"Leave it with me," I said.

The simple fact was, the ship wasn't kitted out to deal with a rodent infestation. There were measures in place to prevent it in port, but who expected to get infested in space? The galley had a few humane traps, more for the reassurance of the guests than anything else, but there was no way to know for sure where the mice had gone.

Unless we could drive them into the traps.

"Mac, call up the galley and see if we can borrow their traps. And get some peanut butter."

"Feeling peckish, Chief?"

"No, but I bet Mrs Fletcher's mice are."

Over the course of the next hour, Mac got and prepped the traps while I studied the layout of the ventilation system. That was probably where the mice had escaped into, so that was where we had to start.

George was not happy when I tried to put him into a baby blue jacket with butterfly-shaped buttons on the front.

"Quit squirming," I said. He twisted in my grasp and his baggy skin slipped through my fingers. In his haste to get away, he scrabbled across my forearms and left a trail of red oozing scratches in his wake. "Dammit, George!"

I heard scrabbling from beneath my bed, and knelt down to see his yellow eyes peering out from between the storage boxes underneath. He hissed as I reached towards him.

"It's for your own good," I said. "It can get cold in the vents." George backed further in.

"Look," I said, wondering why I was bothering to negotiate with a cat, "if you do this for me I'll make sure the knitted horrors don't go with you to your new home. Your new owners will buy you things. I can't guarantee you'll like them, but you should be fine as long as they don't crochet."

George huffed out a breath and tucked his legs underneath him, obviously settling down for a lengthy protest.

"Fine then, no more playing fair."

I backed away and headed to the kitchen counter. I reached for the box of biscuits and gave them a good shake, then put them aside to wash and dress the scratches.

When I turned back George was sat behind me, staring intently at the box of biscuits with his tail lashing like a particularly bad-tempered snake.

"After the jacket goes on," I said. George's tail whipped as I approached with biscuits in one hand and the jacket in the other, but a pile of biscuits on the floor was enough to distract him while I pulled the jacket sleeves over one paw at a time and buttoned him up.

I took him to Mrs Fletcher's cabin in the box - no point in humiliating the poor feline any more than he had to be. When I let him out the reaction was immediate. He started scratching and pawing at the ventilation cover.

"Mr Munroe, I have to ask. You won't let that creature eat my mice?"

"We have humane traps waiting for them, ma'am," I said. "George is just here as encouragement."

"As long as they don't get hurt."

"Ma'am."

I prised the cover off and George disappeared. I crawled in after him.

All of the ship's access points had automatic lighting, which flicked on just ahead of me as George sniffed his way down the corridor. I tapped my radio headset.

"He's heading starboard. Close off access past vent 47 in case he changes his mind." The vent I'd just passed clicked shut. Nothing but air would get past.

We went on like that for what seemed like half a day. George picked a direction, I followed, and Mac closed the vents behind us. My elbows and knees ached, and soon I was covered in dust. I was just recovering from a sneezing fit when George froze, crouched, and wiggled his bottom. Tiny shapes skittered away as he pounced.

"Mac, they're heading towards the access point to vent 92. Get the traps ready." George had raced ahead, pouncing and bouncing in the confined space.

"I see them." Mac's voice was tinny in my ear. "They're moving through the vent. I count five. Closing the access now."

Ahead of me another vent closed, separating George and the mice. George gave a yowl of protest but I was prepared. I rattled the small tub of biscuits in my pocket and, reluctantly, he came back over to eat them.

"Don't tell the captain," I said as I rubbed George between the ears. "We're not supposed to eat in here."

"I think I have a solution to our animal problem, sir. Licences."

The Captain waited for me to continue.

"The senior residents want company, and they're sneaking animals on board to get it. I've heard reports of there being, at various times, a fish tank, parrots, and a miniature poodle."

"And housekeeping saw none of this?"

"The senior residents can be crafty, sir. Mrs Fletcher hid her mice in the wardrobe knowing full well none of the housekeeping staff would look there." It didn't explain how they'd missed a dog or a very vocal parrot, but that wasn't the point.

"And how would licences help, Munroe? This is a cruise liner, not a zoo."

"If we make it clear certain animals are allowed, if the owner has a licence, I think a lot less of the senior residents will be inclined to hide their pets from us. They get the company, and we can monitor what comes on board and make sure they're not a risk to the ship. Fish tanks to be inspected by the engineering crew, to make sure there'll be no damage to the electrics if they leak, that sort of thing."

"You might be on to something there. If we charge for the licence, it can cover associated costs. And it will discourage any casual travellers from bringing pets along. All right Munroe, I'll consider it."

"Yes, sir. And if it does go ahead, I'd like to apply for a licence for George."

"You want to keep Miss Davenport's ugly cat?"

"Yes sir. He's been a great help, and if something like this happens again, well we can't guarantee no one else will have a liking for rodents."

The captain laughed. "Well played, Munroe. Very well, you can keep the cat."

That evening, Miss Davenport arrived on my doorstep in a floor length dress, obviously on her way to one of the liner's many functions.

"I got George a present," she said. "To celebrate." She handed over a folded orange bundle which turned out to be a miniature set of engineering overalls, straight off one of the teddy bears from the gift shop. "Wouldn't want him to get cold."

George went into the overalls with surprisingly little fuss. He butted against my face, which I assumed meant he appreciated the warmth. Or at least that this time it wasn't a knitted pastel jacket.

"I hear the mice were dealt with humanely," Miss Davenport said. "Well handled, dear, I knew you'd manage it."

"George doesn't seem to be a very good mouser," I said. "But he earned his keep."

"Of course he did, dear." Miss Davenport patted the back of my hand. "Why do you think I released the little buggers in the first place? Now I really must dash, dinner plans."

With that she walked away. George rolled on his back on the couch and started to purr.

C.L. Holland is a British writer of fantasy and science fiction, and winner of Writers of the Future. Sometimes she writes poetry under an assumed name. She has a BA in English with Creative Writing, and MA in English, and likes to learn things for fun. She lives with her long-suffering partner and two cats who don't understand why they can't share her lap with the laptop.

More at clholland.weebly.com

Last House, Lost House

First published in Short & Twisted: Fairy Tale (June 2012)

William Ledbetter

Gyllene stopped in the middle of the crumbled asphalt road, raised her dusty goggles and stared at the rambling, two-story stone house. She'd selected the unmarked road because it had high banks on either side and was surrounded by dead, but unburned trees, all helping to break the wind from the approaching storm. The standing trees had been surprise enough, but a house?

Lightning crackled overhead and a powerful gust blasted her with wind-driven grit, nearly blowing her over. She reseated her goggles and using her walking stick, shifted the weight off her splinted right leg, but couldn't stop looking at the house. Even its windows were intact. In an area that hadn't burned, there could be people inside. She took a step forward and her pulse raced. She suddenly couldn't suck enough air through the rags wrapped tightly around her nose and mouth.

"Calm down, Gyllene. They might kill you," she mumbled into her rags. "Or worse, they might take your food and not kill you." She clutched the hidden pocket in her coat that contained a few remaining handfuls of feed corn she'd found in an old silo. As she stared, the wind strengthened abruptly and the house vanished in a swirling dust cloud.

"No!" she yelled into the howling storm and stumbled toward the driveway, but after a few steps, the dust cleared and the house returned. It hadn't been a hallucination. She trembled all over and the heartbeat pounding in her ears nearly drown out the wind.

"Screw the corn," she mumbled and started up the concrete drive at her top limping speed. After not seeing a living person in months — maybe more than a year — she would gladly swap her last food for a five minute conversation.

She made it halfway up the sidewalk leading to the front door, then paused at four brick steps that separated the walk into two levels. Steps were always tough, but instead of risking a fall, she bypassed them by going up what was once a sloped lawn and pushing her way past the long-dead rose bushes. There she yanked to a halt.

She looked down at the split and frayed composite bone protruding trough the faux skin above her ankle splint. It snagged and collected everything from leaves to string and had started looking like a bird's nest. She would've removed and discarded the useless leg long ago, but leaving the attachment interface open to dust and elements would have insured never using it again.

She tried bending down to grab the thorny branch, but couldn't reach it, so she balanced on her good leg long enough to leverage the walking stick under the vine and yank up. The brittle plant shattered and she lurched forward, nearly falling.

She managed the remaining sidewalk and one short step up to the porch without further problems, then pounded on the front door.

"Hello!"

Dried and peeling lacquer sloughed off with each bang of her fist, but the heavy wooden door was still solid and sturdy. It also had no glass, only a peep-hole and a brass knocker, which she tried.

Lightning laced through the brown sky and the temperature dropped noticeably. The storm wouldn't carry rain, but her makeshift mask would never handle the thick dust and if she inhaled too much into her still human lungs, she'd die a long and painful death.

She considered breaking one of the front windows, but decided to check the back door instead and stumped her way around the side of the house.

The wind wasn't as bad in the back and she saw signs of post-impact habitation. Dozens of tree stumps with axe marks dotted the acre behind the house, but the large rectangular pool excited her the most. It contained no water, but was nearly half filled with discarded food packaging. No cardboard boxes – those would've been burned as fuel during the twenty-month winter – but there were piles of cans, jars and plastic containers.

She turned toward the house, hoping to see faces peering at her from the large rear windows, but they were empty and black, so she gave the pool a closer examination. The pool walls visible above the trash were still vivid blue and shone with an unnatural intensity that made her squint behind the dusty goggles. She seldom saw colors like that anymore. But the once bright consumer packages filling the pool bottom were sun-bleached and scoured by dust and windborne debris. Everything had been there awhile. She didn't see anything new.

Her shoulders slumped and she felt suddenly tired. "Looks like your precious corn will be safe after all, Gyllene."

The wind shifted, causing dust columns to rise from the pool as lightning laced the brown sky above, so she once again started toward the house. It was large and while in better shape than most she'd seen since the impact, had suffered some damage. A satellite TV dish dangled from the roof by cables and dozens of the large clay roof tiles lay smashed on the ground. Debris clogged the gutters and dust had drifted in all the corners.

She picked her way through the overturned metal lawn furniture in the outdoor cooking area and approached the French doors leading to the patio. Several outer layers of the double-paned glass were broken, but the doors were still locked. She pounded on the door and yelled again, but heard only the raising wind.

After pulling a hatchet from her bag, she smashed both layers of glass closest to the door handle. When no gunshots followed, she unlocked the door and went inside.

She paused near the door, letting her eyes adjust to the dim interior. A layer of thick dust covering the kitchen floor and a whiff of that musty smell associated with the long dead, told her she was still alone.

Since finding companionship seemed unlikely, she shifted into scavenger mode. Her synthetic body and remaining natural organs required much less food and water than a normal person, but even that proved harder and harder to find. And from what she could already see, this house probably had none.

The doors had been removed from the cabinets and pantry, revealing familiar empty shelves. Since the house hadn't burned in the worldwide fires, there was a good chance the survivors who filled the pool with trash had been the house's owners. The twenty-month winter had eventually grown too cold for cutting wood outside, but the occupants probably hadn't frozen, because the expensive wooden flooring hadn't been burned. They had most likely starved to death, which meant little chance of finding hidden food stashes. With plenty of time and nowhere to go while the storm raged, she explored.

The walking stick and shattered leg made it nearly impossible to move with silence, but she could still use caution. She examined the dust on the floor before leaving the kitchen. It wasn't built up by years of disuse, but had come from outside. She could see it in the air and heard the wind whistling through a broken window somewhere deeper in the house. No human footprints marred the dust, only small animals, and even those were not fresh. The only new prints were oddly round. At first glance they looked like dust-off spots made by some winged insect, but they were arranged in regular alternating patterns like foot steps. They actually resembled the marks left by her walking stick, round with a slight drag mark, only softer, with no sharply defined edges. She tried to imagine what animal might leave such tracks, but couldn't.

The house had been opulent, still displaying imported rugs, original oil paintings, crystal lighting and silver vases. The custom made furniture had probably been burned as fuel along with the kitchen cabinet doors in the obviously well-used fireplace, but she saw remnants of a tastefully designed décor.

Many brands and designers were painfully familiar. She'd used them in her own home. The house she'd been so proud and pleased to show off. She'd always been so eager to impress her friends with her things, her life and her husband, who brought home huge paychecks for simply moving other people's money around. It had all meant nothing, but she'd been very happy.

She only glanced at the family pictures on the mantle. The healthy, bright smiling faces in their ski gear, or standing on beaches and even one in Christmas sweaters, were too painful. They threatened to resurrect memories she'd spent years trying to bury.

And also like her home from that previous life, the house was probably over five-thousand square feet if the second floor matched the lower level. She'd saved that for last. Mostly because stairs were difficult for her, but also because she hadn't found bodies yet, so they would be up there. She also found the odd round prints on the carpeted steps.

"Hello!" she yelled again. Nobody answered.

Going up the stairs was easiest backward, on her butt, with the mask pulled over her nose to filter out the dust she stirred up. With each three or four steps, she'd pause to let the cloud settle, and to listen.

She found the broken window at the top of the stairwell. At one point someone had duct-taped plastic over the hole, but that now hung below the window by a single strip. It had once been a pretty stained glass window. Bits of color still glittered from their lead mounts.

She also found the bodies. The people, she corrected herself. Many more than she'd expected. Five adults lay in a neat row in the game room beside the pool table. All were covered with dust, but only four of them had decayed. The fifth, a petite woman, looked perfectly intact. She wasn't mummified or gnawed by animals, but instead looked as if she were asleep.

Gyllene gasped and dropped to the floor, nearly cracking her head against the big table. Her heart pounded as she scrambled across the floor to the woman. With shaking hands she unfastened the tight jeans and then tugged, grunted and pulled until she got them off. She ran her hand up and down the cold right leg, then stopped and sighed. It was going to be too small. Just to make sure, she felt above the knee until she found the studs to trip the joint locks, then squeezed hard until the leg detached at the hip with a mechanical click. She looked at the numbers inside the joint and cursed. The attachment point was one size too small.

With a heavy sigh, she left the leg on the floor and struggled back to her feet. Almost all the women she knew had opted for the same tall, leggy body Gyllene had purchased, but in order to not shock their kids or relatives, a rare few had ordered custom frames that resembled perfected versions of their own natural bodies. She had of course found one of those.

She looked around and froze for a second when she saw her reflection in the mirror above the wet bar. Then she laughed. Two years before the impact, her cybernetic metamorphoses had cost her three weeks of agony and enough cash to buy an average house, all to make her eternally beautiful. She and her rich friends had finally beaten the last daunting foe of human vanity; the betrayal of an aging body.

The thing staring back at Gyllene from the mirror was clad in stiff dirt-colored rags, the guaranteed lustrous synthetic hair was matted into a near solid mass below the cord holding her ponytail and a permanent sooty stripe coated the skin between her goggles and mask. What would her friends think of her now?

Thunder rumbled long in the north, vibrating the house and reminding Gyllene that she now had a different life. Feeling heavier and more tired than should be possible, she shuffled and thumped down a hallway that must lead to the bedrooms.

The first two rooms were empty, but for scattered clothes and dirty mattresses on the floor. The wooden bed frames and furniture long gone. The third room had no bodies either, but made her pause. It was filled with stuffed animals and toys.

A smiling sun had been painted on one wall and on a wall hook near the brass bed hung a sky blue robe covered in yellow ducks. With a groan and a suddenly tight throat she scrambled across the room to grab the robe. Her own five year old daughter had the same one. It disappeared, along with Kimberly, her husband and her expensive house, when a tidal wave taller than the Empire State Building erased Florida. She knew they were gone, because after the twenty-month winter, she'd made a year-long trek to stand on the new coastline, fifty miles north of where she used to live.

She stumbled back into the hallway, yanked down the mask and buried her face in the dusty robe. Though most likely her imagination, she thought she could smell the faint trace of a little girl fresh from the bath. The memories she'd ignored and hid and shoved into dark corners, all exploded in her head like July Fourth fireworks. Kimberly giggling as she was tickled by her father. Her face filled with stunned delight as she held a three-day old yellow kitten. Even flashes from her own childhood, and wedding and college. Her baby, her husband, her parents and sister. All gone. It was too much.

Her sobs echoed in the hallway and were all the more painful because she couldn't actually cry. Her computer regulated cybernetic systems deemed tears a waste of precious resources in her dehydrated state. She moaned and pounded the wall with her fist, but nothing eased the pain. Nothing ever would.

Powerful winds strained to push the house down and though the structure creaked and moaned, it did not fall. The stone walls were strong and might stand for decades, but that only meant no one would see or care when they did collapse.

Gyllene pulled her mask up, then gently folded the robe and placed it in her bag. With the duckies out of sight, she was also able to systematically tuck her memories into places where they couldn't hurt her. She took a long shuddering breath and proceeded to explore the rest of the rooms.

After finding a home theater, a small gym, and two more bedrooms, she paused before going further down the hall. Deep shadows hid the end, but a cluster of small, dim lights tantalized her. She pulled the flashlight from her bag, cranked it a dozen times and pointed it into the darkness.

The beam revealed a toppled accent table and a dust covered axe laying on the floor near a closed, beat up wooden door. She approached slowly. The door's very existence was odd enough, since the doors from other rooms were gone, as were the wooden baseboards, trim and stair railing, but when she tried the knob, it was also locked.

Deep hack marks near the lock and doorknob had no doubt been made by the discarded axe, but the tiny lights had come from weak sunlight streaming through five bullet holes clustered mid-way up the door. Those holes were splintered outward. They had come from the inside. Gyllene stepped to one side and pounded on the door.

Last House, Lost House

"Hello?"

Only wind whistling through the broken window answered. She cranked her flashlight again and checked the floor. Hundreds of the little round spots had cleared away most of the dust in front of the door and revealed dried blood spatters and smears. She looked back down the hall and could see the round prints everywhere.

Carefully avoiding the duckie robe, she fished around in her bag to find her large screwdriver. Knocking the doorknob off took a dozen hits from the axe's blunt end, but one hard strike on the screwdriver broke the lock. Thunder rattled the house again as she shoved the door open.

Dim light from three windows revealed a man's body on the floor between the door and a large bed. An automatic pistol spilled from one slack hand and the top of his head had been splattered in a wide cone across the carpet. He had a cybernetic body, but one glance told her his legs would be worthless. The guy had once been at least six and a half feet tall. Too big, the attachment points would be all wrong.

The rest of the room was even more sad. Two mummified children, girls by the look of their long hair, were covered by a blanket and had sunk deep into the collapsed mattress. Their mother sat in a seat next to the bed, a neat bullet hole in her forehead and the back of her head plastered to the chair by petrified gore. She too had a synthetic body and looked to be the perfect size match for the shattered leg.

Gyllene felt no elation. Instead, she sat on the edge of the bed, ignoring the puff of dust and looked around. Empty prescription bottles sat on the night stand and a pile of discarded food boxes lay in a corner. Jugs and buckets, also empty, sat in a neat row under the windows.

This had been their last stand. Toward the end, the parents had probably put their own children's needs ahead of the others in the house, hoarding the last of the food and water in their room. But it had been too late. Their generosity to neighbors or extended family or friends had depleted what little they had.

At least they'd been together at the end. This mother hadn't been halfway across the country at a bachelorette party in Vegas. And also unlike Gyllene, these people had the strength and good sense to end their suffering when food and hope had dwindled, probably minutes after their children's deaths. It was right and proper.

She bent down and picked up the gun. It was heavy. During her years of wandering since the long winter, she'd never carried a gun. She'd told herself it was because she refused to take another person's life – they were too rare and precious now – but holding the gun she realized there had been another reason.

With a quivering hand she touched the dusty blanket covering the little girls and the dry sobs came again, but this time they were weak and passionless. She clawed the mask from her face, no longer caring about the dust, and pulled the robe from her bag. With robe and pistol clutched to her perfect, oh-so-natural looking breasts, she rocked back and forth on the squeaking bed. It was time. It was past time.

"Thank you for unlocking that door," a soft baritone voice said from her right.

She swung the gun around at a dust-covered teddy bear standing in the open doorway. It was large for teddy bears, probably more than two feet tall, and it blinked at her.

"I guessed why they never came out," it said. "But I didn't know for sure. I wish I could've been with Celia at the end. Being near me made her happy. Or at least less sad."

"Oh," Gyllene sighed and lowered the gun. "You're just a toy."

"My name is Thaddeus, I'm a *MyBear*. That's trademarked by the way. But Celia couldn't say Thaddeus so she called me Taddius or usually just Taddie. I didn't mind at all."

It took several steps into the room and stopped a few feet from Gyllene's knee. "I'm what grownups called a level two adaptive AI. Not only can I do things like read to children, I can actually pretend with them. I can help make up stories and adventures, while keeping them safe and healthy."

Gyllene remembered the commercials and news stories about the AI companions calling an ambulance when a child was hurt, helping find lost kids and even saving a family from a fire. They had been the perfect guilt-free electronic babysitters, much better than parking the kids in front of a video screen. She'd even considered buying one for Kimberly.

"How...I mean...your batteries?"

"My systems are very efficient. As long as I go dormant near a window, even faint sunlight will keep my batteries charged. Did you come into Celia's room?"

Gyllene nodded.

"Then you must've triggered my motion detectors. I would have said 'hello' sooner, but it took twelve minutes for my systems to boot and run diagnostics after being in power conservation mode."

She shrugged and hugged the robe to her face again.

"Did you know Celia?" the bear asked.

"No," she said. "But I had a little girl like Celia once." Then she felt silly for explaining herself to a toy bear. "Look, could you go away? I have something I need to do. Alone."

Thaddeus Bear stared at her for a second, then said, "Can I go with you when you leave? I've been very lonely."

"We'll talk about it later."

"I know you think I'm a kid's toy, but I'm also a very good companion for lonely adults too."

She held the gun up and looked at it. "I don't think you can help me, Taddie."

"Did you know that my company interface satellite survived the debris field thrown up by the impact?"

Gyllene blinked at him. "What?"

"MyBear Incorporated was able to update and perform diagnostics on their products using a satellite interface. They haven't sent any updates since the impact, but I've heard from twenty-two other companions via the network. Most of them are alone like me, but nine of them are still with people. Seven in the North America and two in Japan."

"Seven," she mumbled. "Here? Where?"

"I'm not sure. The GPS system no longer functions. But they're with people somewhere here in North America."

Gyllene stared at the bear for several minutes, then laid the gun on the bed and turned her attention to the dead woman.

"What was Celia's mom's name?"

"Elizabeth."

With a nod, she stuffed the robe back into her bag and struggled to her feet.

Gyllene paused in the road and looked back at the house as Thaddeus struggled to catch up.

"I think I'm going to have to carry you," she said when he finally waddled up next to her. "You walk well, but your legs are just too short to keep up."

"That's okay. I'm very light so children can carry me and I like to be carried. And I especially like to be hugged."

"Me too," she said and scooped him up into a big hug.

They started north, leaving the burned ruins of Raleigh behind them. Years before, Gyllene heard a rumor of survivors in the Allegheny Mountains. That might be worth exploring.

"So by your pace, I assume Elizabeth's legs fit well?" Taddie asked.

"They're just right," she said. "And thank you."

The bear turned to look at her. "For what?"

"For the tale about the other bears. You make up really good stories," Gyllene said.

The bear's soft muzzle stretched into a smile.

"Celia always liked them too."

William Ledbetter is a Nebula Award winner with more than fifty speculative fiction stories and non-fiction articles published in markets such as *Fantasy & Science Fiction*, *Jim Baen's Universe*, *Writers of the Future*, *Escape Pod*, *Daily SF*, the SFWA blog, and *Ad Astra*.

A space and technology geek since childhood, he's spent most of his non-writing career in the aerospace and defense industry and is a graduate of the Launch Pad Astronomy workshop.

He belongs to SFWA and the National Space Society of North Texas, and administers the Jim Baen Memorial Short Story Award contest for Baen Books and the National Space Society. He's also the Science Track coordinator for Fencon and a consulting editor at *Heroic Fantasy Quarterly*.

He lives near Dallas with his wife and three spoiled cats.

More at www.williamledbetter.com

Softly Into the Morning

First published in Pseudopod #485 (April 2016)

L. D. Colter

The shimmering glow of Sol appeared at the edge of Mercury. Jack watched the growing crescent of fiery gold from the best seat in the house, the center console of the large forward window. The privilege had been coincidental, the consequence of a flight engineer needing less space for screens than the captain or navigator.

The window tinting couldn't keep pace with the increasing light and Jack's eyes watered from the intensely focused brightness. Still, he couldn't turn away from that life-giving light amidst all this vast darkness. Dawn had always affected Jack. At home, in the Florida Keys, he never failed to be up in time to see the sunrise. And today he was closer to the sun than any human in history.

"Time to earn our pay," Wainwright said. The captain drifted near Jack watching the spectacle, but tugged himself now into his chair and snapped his harness into place. A muscle twitching below one eye was the only telltale that the unflappable Edward Wainwright felt as tense as his crew.

Jack knew that earning their pay was the least of their worries; if the sails didn't deploy, it was doubtful any of them would live to see Earth again.

Orbital pull continued to draw the ship from planetary shadow into full sunlight and the window, at last, tinted to black. Jack hoped the rest of the ship's special designs responded more efficiently than the window, especially the plating on the sun shields protecting the exterior of the ship.

Budget concerns had reduced the ship's design to a small, two-level cylindrical capsule that had no hydroponic backup and little margin for error on fuel. While still under construction, the launch date had been moved up a full month to beat the competition, making it almost certain that still more corners had been cut.

"Confirm coordinates for target window," Wainwright said.

"Coordinates confirmed," Yeung replied from her navigation console at Jack's right.

"Deploy sails on my mark." Wainwright stared at the stream of green numbers ticking across his console. Jack's fingers hovered over his keyboard as Wainwright counted down. "Ready in three, two, one, mark."

Jack entered the deployment code. For a moment nothing happened, then distant asynchronous clunks sounded on either side of the bridge as the sail panel doors blasted away into space. He turned to the starboard window and held his breath for the longest seconds of his life. The silver Mylar fabric mushroomed into view.

He looked out the port window in time to see the other sail deploy. The material briefly filled the windows, obscuring the black sky before flaring back on either side of the ship into huge silver wings.

An unrestrained whoop erupted from Jack. Wainwright and Yeung joined in. Within the hour those beautiful sails would begin charging their solar drive. When the drive was at full capacity, they would leave orbit and travel at a vastly increased speed for the next thirty days. Most importantly, the increased speed would prevent them from running out of oxygen, food, and fuel somewhere between Venus and Earth.

Wainwright unclipped his harness and floated from his seat. He pulled himself to Jack's console and reached out a hand. Jack took it in a firm handshake.

"Congratulations, Major Spalter," Wainwright said. He hauled himself forward and extended his hand to Karen. "Congratulations,

Major Yeung." Karen shook the captain's hand, grinning her wide, mid-westerner's smile that always made Jack smile too.

"What the hell…" Wainwright said.

Jack swiveled his chair to look out the small window where Wainwright was staring. The panel that had covered the starboard sail compartment was spinning past, end over end, still moving at explosive speed. It was close enough to the window to see that one corner of the panel was nothing but ragged metal. The trajectory would slam it straight into the ship.

"Oh my God," Jack murmured. Wainwright tore his gaze from the window and Jack saw him flail belatedly for a handhold.

The panel hit just above the window, hard enough to throw Jack forward into his harness. The collision sounded like a car crashing into a trash can with Jack inside the can. From the corner of his vision he saw Karen pulling up data while still righting herself.

Jack panned to an external camera, finding the damage to the sun shield at the point of impact to be the least of their worries. The panel was rebounding, and was headed directly for the starboard sail.

Jack's heart skipped a beat as the panel hit the sail. It struck near the upper horizontal strut of the kite-like skeleton, leaving the strut dangling like a broken arm as the panel slashed down through the Mylar.

The fabric flapped ineffectively around the gaping hole. Jack watched the panel through the hole as it spun away into its own orbit of Mercury.

The captain should have been checking damage readouts, double-checking vector and velocity, making decisions on whether they should try and retract sails. Nothing.

Jack turned, searching for Wainwright. He found him drifting at the ceiling. His head hung back, his ear unnaturally close to his right shoulder-blade. There was a bony bulge on the side of his neck where no vertebrae should have protruded.

There was no time to think about him now, or the unfairness of the accident occurring during the few moments Wainwright had been unharnessed. Jack released himself from his chair in one quick motion, grabbed the back of the captain's chair and pulled himself into it, clipping in again.

"External cameras three and four inoperative," he reported in a voice that was too crisp and steady to be his own. "Right sail damaged. Left sail intact. All instruments online except starboard sail angle controls."

"Port thruster, 102.032 pounds of thrust now," Yeung said louder than necessary.

"Firing port thruster." Jack executed the maneuver, using a small portion of their precious re-entry fuel.

"Check calculations," Yeung said.

Jack focused on the numbers flowing across the screen. He pulled up the data from just prior to the collision and did the comparison. "Coordinates correct. Nav systems functioning properly."

Karen's shoulders visibly relaxed. "Orbit is stable," she confirmed.

She twisted and looked over her shoulder for a long moment at Wainwright floating above her. She must have seen him from the corner of her eye after the impact but exercised enough discipline not to look until now.

Jack's brain refused to wrap around the idea that Wainwright could be dead when he had been alive just a moment ago even though Jack had experienced sudden death before. Denise. According to the doctor, she'd died of sudden hemorrhage from a congenital cerebral aneurysm.

Jack felt as if he stood in the kitchen with her again. Her last words were mundane, telling him the dishwasher had been run. Her eyes tightened in thoughtful inward reflection, her mouth pursed as if about to ask a question, and she collapsed to the floor. Neither of them had known she had a time-bomb in her head.

Jack felt disconnected from the present   the memory dredged from a pool deep in his mind, pulled to the surface like a fish on a hook. He shook free of his recollection with difficulty.

"How the hell did that sail door hit us?" he said, tearing his eyes from Wainwright's body.

"My guess is a malfunction in the bolt explosives," Yeung said, also turning away from Wainwright with apparent effort. "The right side of the door must have blown later than the left, and the combined speeds of the ship and the panel caused it to hit with a hell of a force." Karen's voice went soft and distant, as did her eyes. "Just like what happened to Maria."

Jack looked hard at her. Perhaps delayed shock was affecting them both. Psychological manifestations of any level were the number one concern when you were traveling in a tin can through outer space.

"Who's Maria?" Jack asked cautiously.

Karen looked at him. She seemed herself. Muted, but okay.

"A friend of mine in college," she said, "killed by a rock the size of a grapefruit when we were on a road trip. It came down the canyon. The windshield didn't even slow it down. Flattened one side of her head and never touched me. Odd. I haven't thought of her in a couple of years."

Their captain was dead and their ship was damaged   what the hell were they both doing reminiscing about the past? Maybe it was the brain's way of categorizing an unexpected death.

"We need to take care of Wainwright and start on projections," Jack said. "Then see what we can do about that sail."

Karen nodded.

It didn't take Jack long to realize that the projections sucked.

They were only a little more than half way through their six month guinea pig run to Mercury and back. The modified chemical fuel had been used up getting them well into solar orbit in record time and now they needed every bit of super-accelerated solar drive to make it back to Earth on the regular fuel before their life-support resources ran out.

He looked at the numbers again and shook his head. "I knew they'd screw things up when they bumped up the launch deadline."

"There are a lot of variables," Karen said. "It's possible that moving the launch date up had nothing to do with the panel malfunction."

Jack wasn't buying it. When government funding for NASA dried up, private companies had formed overnight. Hyde Exploration Industries and Virgin Space emerged as the front-runners. The competition for patents was fierce, especially for the new solar sail technology that promised nearly unlimited acceleration. HEI had won the launch race to test the sails at the highest solar intensity yet, but at what cost?

"I'll suit up," Jack said. He unclipped and pulled himself to the ladder that would take him from the upper level containing the bridge and galley to the lower level with the sleeping cubicles, medical bay, engine access, and airlock. He moved down the rails quickly, feet floating free. The repair tape they had wouldn't completely cover the gaping hole in the sail, but hopefully it would patch the Mylar well enough to get the solar drive charged.

Karen followed him down. "You're staying here," she said. "I'll go out."

"Forget it," Jack said, pushing off the ladder to the nearest handhold and reaching for the pressure suit closet by the airlock bay. "I'm the mechanical engineer and those sails are my baby."

Karen laid a hand on Jack's outstretched arm. "I know they are. I also know you did more training on the sails than Wainwright and

I combined. That's why you need to be on the bridge, where you can see everything. Any monkey can stick a piece of tape on a hole."

Jack hesitated, but Karen was right. "All right," he conceded. "I'll get the tape for you."

He moved down the hall to a small tool locker near the engine access while Karen suited up. The tape glittered with the same Mylar covering as the sails. They had one roll, thirty feet by six inches; like everything else, the minimum HEI thought necessary for a safety margin.

Karen was reaching for her helmet when Jack returned. "Do you want this tied on?" he asked her, holding up the roll.

"Let me try something," Karen said, taking it from him. She pushed her hand into the cardboard hole in the center and wriggled her gloved fingers to get the knuckle joints through. The result was a thick, shiny bracelet. She swung her arm up and down. "Safe and secure."

Jack helped Karen with her helmet and tied a pair of heavy scissors and a portable welder to her belt. He opened the inner airlock door. "Be safe out there," he said, "it's a long way down."

Karen nodded and gave him her big smile and a thumbs-up. Jack waited until she was safely tethered then shut the inner door. He pressed a second button and heard the droning buzz of the outer door alarm. Through the porthole he saw the big, bay door open onto the black space beyond. Karen re-clipped to the exterior tether and stepped out into space. Jack closed the door behind her, pushed off hard, grabbed the ladder rails, and hurried to the bridge.

Karen had already angled the ship to keep the sun off that side, and from the starboard window he watched her ease out in full shadow. She maneuvered onto the unbroken lower strut of the sail. Watching Karen out there in space, the unfamiliar sensation of being the only person on the ship tickled at Jack like one of those hard to locate itches.

It was difficult to leave the window, but he had his own job to do. He tugged himself to his console and harnessed in. Opening the comm channel, he heard Karen's fishbowl breath. "How's it going out there, Karen?"

"Good so far," came back the static-filled reply. "The lower horizontal strut looks fine. Vertical-strut looking good too. Starting up the pegs to the upper horizontal strut now."

"Okay, just like we said. Weld that break as straight as possible first, then work on the tear."

"Roger that."

Karen came into view of one of the remaining functional cameras. She had her work cut out trying to get the arm straight, then hold it in place one-handed while she welded. The fabric was as light as it was strong, but twenty square meters of it would be awkward for anyone.

Jack busied himself with figuring the best placement of the tape they had available. It wasn't hard. The tear was L-shaped, roughly one hundred and twenty feet long   patch two feet out of every eight. He passed on the info to Karen then began calculating the amount of change in solar capacity in case she couldn't get that strut welded straight.

He'd just finished the calculations when the sensation of being watched tickled between his shoulder blades. Turning, he searched the ceiling where Wainwright died. He saw nothing there. Jack turned back to his work but the muscles of his upper back wouldn't relax. The comm headset crackled in his ear.

"What?" Karen asked.

"Negative," Jack replied. "I didn't say anything."

Karen's deep, puffing respirations filled the receiver on Jack's headset. "Maria?" Karen said. Goosebumps prickled Jack's arms.

"Hey, Karen. What's going on out there? You okay?"

"You want what, Maria?"

"Karen?" Jack paused. "Major Yeung. Respond."

No answer.

"Karen, check your O2 valve. Look for kinks in the tubing. Make sure your reservoir is okay."

With the headset still on, Jack unharnessed and used the hand holds to gain the starboard window again. Karen had already welded the strut in place but hung from it now by one hand. She had turned away from the sail and reached out into space with her other hand.

"Dad, wait, I'll help you," Karen said.

Four months off-planet was bad enough, but Jack had been warned that stepping out of the craft into the vastness of space could unhinge the strongest of personalities. He watched in horror as Karen reached down and struggled with the clip to her tether line.

"Karen!" Jack shouted. "You're hallucinating. Listen to me, Karen!"

"Wait, Dad," Karen said to the father Jack knew had died five years ago. He had fallen off a ladder as he tried to clean the rain gutters. Karen had witnessed it.

Jack's guts clenched and a wave of nausea assailed him as Karen unclipped and dropped the line. She drifted up about a meter before her collar snagged on a climbing peg on the vertical strut. She didn't seem to notice. Both arms reached forward and her feet kicked slightly, as if she was running. "I will," she said.

Helpless, he watched as his friend and shipmate reached up and twisted her helmet. "Karen, God damn it, it's a hallucination!" Jack yelled. Emotion broke his voice. "Don't do it!" But it was already done.

Jack pressed his hands against the sides of the window, as if he could push his way out to her. She didn't explode, like in the movies. Her blood wouldn't boil either, though the water on any exposed mucous surface like her tongue or eyes might briefly. He watched her hang for about thirty seconds before her head slumped forward from oxygen deprivation. Her heart would stop soon. She had maybe up to four minutes before permanent brain death. Far less time than it would take Jack to reach her.

Jack smashed one hand against the wall. The itch of loneliness became a hole as big as the one gaping in the sail. He should have gone out there instead of her. At the least, he should have gone with her to help out, despite the regulations that said one person on the ship at all times.

He pressed his forehead to the cool metal wall. He couldn't lose it now. He had to focus on survival. And the first step was to tape up the sail.

Jack didn't know why he turned on the comm in his helmet. There was no one left to talk to, but the sound of his breath echoing in the mic made him feel better. He double and triple checked his tether and clip before opening the outer airlock door. The air hissed out into the vacuum of space.

He reached for the spare exterior tether, clipped into it, and unclipped the interior one. Faced with the empty ship behind him and the blackness of space ahead, he couldn't bring himself to close the outer airlock door.

He eased along the side of the ship to the sail and climbed the vertical strut. When he reached the upper horizontal strut Jack saw that Karen had done a bang-up job on the welding despite her hallucinations.

Karen hung above him, eerily reminiscent of Wainwright after the accident. Her foot was within arm's reach. Jack grabbed Karen's boot and pumped up and down trying to shake her collar loose from the peg. On the second try, she came free.

He held her by the ankle, her body floating above him like some obscene balloon. With both feet firmly gripping a peg, Jack pulled Karen down until he could reach her wrist. He wrapped one arm around her and hugged her against his body while he jerked the tape off her wrist and removed the scissors from her belt to tie them to his own. He tried not to look at her face as he worked.

Karen's tether had caught on a nearby peg just above him and it drifted back through the tear like a bicycle handlebar streamer. He reeled the tether in, hooked the clip back on to Karen's belt, and gave her a gentle shove. She floated to the edge of the sail, arms and legs extended toward Jack in a posture of supplication.

Jack turned from the ghastly image and studied the tear. He unrolled the first two feet of tape. Visions of Karen pulling off her helmet kept niggling into his brain. Memories of Wainwright too, floating at the ceiling. He didn't want to think about the dead, he wanted to focus on living, but his thoughts didn't seem to be his own.

Jack peeled the backing from the first few inches of tape and tugged the two sides of the tear together. A memory of his grandmother came to him. She had passed away in the hospital when he was sixteen. It was as if he was there in the hospital with her again. Then came the memory of Henry, the night after their high school football victory party. Jack and his girlfriend had been the first to come across Henry's car wrapped around that tree it was so vivid he could smell the gasoline as it leaked into the ditch. Next came Denise again.

Jack thought he heard something before remembering that the vacuum of space carried no sound. He heard it again. The comm in his helmet crackled loudly. He flinched so violently he nearly lost his hold on the peg. If the tape hadn't been tied to his belt, it would have gone flying into space.

Jack, take that silly thing off so I can see your face.

He heard Denise's voice in his memory as clearly as if she'd just spoken to him. Halloween two years ago, just days before she died.

He saw it as if he stood there with her. His hands drifted toward his helmet of their own accord. An image of Karen doing the same thing came to him and with a start he realized where he was. Sweat dampened the forehead pad of his helmet and made his palms itch. His breath rasped faster, fogging his faceplate despite his oxygen flow.

"Don't you go crazy too," he said aloud to himself. "It's a hallucination. Finish the repairs." He repeated the last phrase silently, like a mantra, over and over, his hands shaking as he hurried. The mantra didn't work; memories of his dead drifted back to him.

He tackled the problem like a mechanical equation. It had been after Wainwright's death that he and Karen started reminiscing about people who had died. Karen had been talking to them when she unclipped and removed her helmet. Why would stress affect them both in the same way? And if it wasn't stress, what was it?

He grabbed the scissors drifting at his chest, cut the tape and pulled the backing the rest of the way off. The strip of paper backing drifted into space as he smoothed the tape up the tear. He moved a few feet higher, judging six feet by his own body length, and pulled another piece of tape free from the roll.

Jack, kiss me one more time. Another memory, just before he left on a training mission. She was afraid that he wouldn't come back to her and was putting off saying goodbye.

He ignored the voice and hurried to anchor the tape. His hands worked on, but Jack sank into a series of memories so real that he could feel Denise's fingers on his flesh. He smelled the lemon shampoo in her hair as she stepped out of the shower and the verdant humidity of their backyard in the Florida Keys where they would sit in the evenings. He was looking at her lying on the floor of their kitchen and he was at her funeral, standing in the rain, her casket at the side of that dark, earthen hole. The images flowed randomly through his wife's life and death. Her death especially.

The thoughts were torn from random stages of his life, grouped so thematically around death and loss that they didn't feel like memories surfacing organically. They felt like something external rummaging through the attic of his life, pulling out the interesting bits for a closer look. That was crazy though, and Jack didn't want to be crazy. It had to be stress. Wainwright's death and Karen's death and the prospect of dying alone in space would be enough to wig anyone out.

He checked his oxygen tank and lines just in case all fine then began his mantra again to focus on finishing the repairs. Whatever had happened to Karen, he was forewarned. It wasn't going to happen to him. These sails were his baby and he was going to fix them and go home. Home became his new mantra.

Jack progressed up the vertical strut and then across the horizontal one, two feet of tape, six foot gap, two feet of tape. All the while, his dead came to visit him and the voices never stopped. Karen. Wainwright. His grandmother. Henry. Denise. They brought the memories with them, visceral and poignant and real as stepping back in time. At times he was so immersed in thoughts of the past that he couldn't see the silver sail in front of his face. And over and over, they all wanted him to do things that would kill him remove his helmet, turn off his O2, untether and float free.

Denise was the hardest to ignore.

Jack pulled the last of the tape from the roll and patched the final section. He glanced over one shoulder at the ship. Karen had calculated the angle before suiting up, just enough change to avoid getting cooked by the sun. She hadn't calculated on dying and Jack's extra time taking over the repairs. The sun was glinting off the middle of the ship. He had to get inside.

Jack. Karen's voice in his head. *Stay for the sunrise.* Karen had said that after a night-training once, knowing how he liked the dawn.

He didn't want to look at Karen's body, but he couldn't help it. She still floated at the end of her tether, holding the position of a baby doll looking to be hugged. He was glad he wasn't close enough to see her eyes.

The right thing would be to take her home for her family to bury, like Wainwright. He didn't move. He stared at her, not wanting to pull her body to him. One of Karen's arms jerked, as if in a parody of a wave.

"What the hell…" he said. It must be rigor mortis but it looked too much like something had gotten inside her and was trying to learn how to work the controls. Whatever it was, it was the last straw. He was leaving Karen and getting the hell out of here. He started down the strut.

Jack, Karen repeated, *stay for the sunrise.*

He couldn't take anymore. He stopped, looking up at her body. "What are you?" he yelled. "Why do you want to kill me?"

His mic clicked again. A short burst of static where there should be none.

What if something *was* out here with him? Something that had witnessed Wainwright dying and now wanted to see death repeated over and over, like a child fascinated with a new toy.

He was done with this. Whether he'd gone crazy, or heaven was a myth and this was where Earth's ghosts congregated, or he was having some bizarre first contact, he needed to get back inside the ship. He needed to get home.

Home. Home. Home. The thought echoed back at him in a chorus of voices.

"The hell I'll take you back," he shouted, suddenly afraid to think of Earth anymore. He scrambled down the pegs, stumbling in his rush and scraping the leg of his suit against the metal. His breath panted loud in his mic. He forced himself to stop and check his suit. No tear.

He reached the lower strut and Karen's tether line. Pulling a knife from his belt, he cut the thick line without hesitation. He didn't watch her body float away.

Jack hurried along the strut to the airlock, wishing he hadn't left the outer door open. He didn't know what might be out here with him, or how it traveled, or where it was now, but if something *was* out here, he sure as hell didn't want it in his ship.

He hauled himself inside hand-over-hand as fast as he could, and unclipped, tossing the line out the door. The second the line drifted out of reach he realized that he hadn't attached himself to the interior tether first. He drifted a foot or so off the floor. The interior tether floated to his left and he made a grab for it. He caught the line between his last two fingers. Sliding up the tether, he found the clip and hooked in with shaking hands.

He banged the airlock control with one fist. The door slid closed.

Jack panted; the sound of his breath ragged and loud in his ears. He pulled himself across the airlock to the interior door and opened it. Closing it behind him, he pushed the switch to reopen the outer door, flushing anything that might have entered the airlock with him back out into space. Jack re-sealed the ship, removed his helmet, fell to his hands and knees, and retched on the floor.

The sails were working beautifully, even the starboard sail with its rag-tag patches. The tape was holding and the solar drive was sixty-two percent charged. Jack's little tin can was floating around Mercury in full sunlight. In a few more hours he could leave orbit, and in forty-three days he'd be able to contact Earth.

The traumas of his space-walk had faded slowly as he busied himself with ship's operations. Jack mulled over the saner explanations to put in his report: oxygen deprivation from an undetected equipment failure or stress-induced hallucinations from crewmates dying. He debated adding the possibility of some unknown gaseous element that had permeated the suit fabric.

A rustling came from the deck below, a scritching, scratching noise that raised the hairs on the back of his neck. He turned from his console where he'd been logging the increase in the solar drive charge.

It couldn't be a rodent. The ship had been combed for four-legged intruders before takeoff. Anything that had evaded the inspection would have died during the periods of oxygen deprivation. Jack drifted to the ladder opening and eased himself down. He stopped at the bottom and listened. He heard it again.

He scanned the space-suit closet and tool locker, but his ears led him further, to the small medical bay where he and Karen had secured Wainwright's body in a thick, black bag. They had planned to move his corpse into refrigeration once she finished the repairs, but after his experience out on the sail Jack had procrastinated, not wanting to deal with another dead body yet.

Wainwright was taller than average for an astronaut, making it hard to fit into the bag. They'd bent his knees, giving the bag the shape of someone relaxing inside. Jack stood in the doorway a long minute, studying the outline of the recumbent form before he entered the medical bay.

He was within a foot of the bag when the body twitched, producing a scratching noise from inside the bag. Jack froze. A wash of adrenaline tightened his hands and cramped his thighs. He thought he heard his mic on the bridge crackle. The movement could have been rigor mortis setting in. The noise on the comm could have been pressure changes in Karen's body forcing air out of her mouth and into the mic embedded in the neck of the suit. Or not.

All of his earlier paranoia came flooding back in a rush. This was no time to rationalize. If there was even a remote chance that an entity had entered the ship with him and that it inhabited Wainwright now, there was only one answer; Wainwright would have to join Karen floating through forever in this God-forsaken stretch of space.

Jack screwed up his nerve, reached forward and released the straps around Wainwright's body. He wrapped his arms about the thick bag. The body inside had already cooled and rigor mortis had indeed started to set in.

Jack struggled down the hallway, vacillating between being fearful of holding him too close and feeling ludicrous for thinking the man's body might be possessed by an alien lifeform. Reaching the airlock, he opened the inner door, gave the bag a push, and hit the button. The door closed with a soft whoosh.

Jack peered through the porthole at the bag covering his friend and captain. He tried to reassure himself that he was doing the right thing. Suddenly, the bag tented up about where Wainwright's arm would've been, as if the arm had jerked in a parody of a wave.

Jack slammed his hand against the airlock control. The alarm buzzed as the outer door slid open and Wainwright's body sucked off the ship. It tumbled slowly through space.

Nauseous and lightheaded, Jack returned to the ladder and climbed to the bridge. He pulled himself into Karen's chair and clipped in. The loss of his last crewmate, even a dead one, gave the ship a palpable emptiness. He didn't know what to believe anymore and had no one left to ask.

"Do something," he muttered to himself. "Stay busy." Jack pulled up the navigation coordinates to double check speed and trajectory, but stared unseeing at the numbers.

Let's go home. Denise. A dozen different iterations of her saying this came to him: hopeful, sensual, enticing. The mic at his station crackled. Jack jerked against his harness with a yell. Fumbling to unclip, he pushed free. His momentum carried him backward to the bulkhead where he gripped a handhold, breathing hard.

Raising a shaking hand, Jack scrubbed it through his hair as if he could untangle the thoughts racing through his mind. "No!" he yelled at the console. "I'll never take you home. Never! Leave me alone!" He heard the crazy in his voice.

One cheap-ass bolt. HEI would never know. Not about the panel malfunction, not about Wainwright's accidental death, and not about Jack's suspicion or delusion that Wainwright's death had attracted whatever had killed Karen and was trying to kill him. They wouldn't know that he believed it had found out about Earth and wanted to go there. He couldn't even send a message from here; a warning not to send other ships.

Alone in his tin can there was no litmus test for his sanity. With the reduced crew, ship's resources were no longer an issue but he couldn't bear another two months like this. And if he wasn't insane then what was inside his head? It might be in the ship, or able to possess a body, or able to follow him through space all the way back to Earth. He had only one option.

Jack strapped into the navigator's chair, fighting to keep his mind blank as he pulled up new coordinates.

Jack. Denise's voice in his head. *What are you doing now?* There were a thousand times she'd said that.

God, he missed her.

"Nothing," he said through gritted teeth. "Nothing." He filled his mind with images of nothing while he found and entered the coordinates.

The front window, still heavily tinted, showed the sun three times larger than seen from Earth. It burned bright and hot. Life-giving hope in the middle of the darkness. The poignancy of it made his eyes sting, but whether from hope or despair he couldn't have said.

Jack, please don't go. A replay of the time he'd volunteered to fly an experimental plane he'd worked on in the Air Force. Denise had been afraid.

Her voice broke his heart, just as it had back then. And just like then, he did what he knew he had to do. He even gave the same answer he had that day.

"It's okay, baby," he said to the real Denise. "I'll see you soon."

The data stream displayed the ship's acceleration. Maybe someone on Earth would be watching the sunrise when he burned.

Due to a varied work background, Liz has harnessed, hitched, and worked draft horses, and worked in medicine, canoe expeditioning, and as a roller-skating waitress. She also knows more about concrete than you might suspect. She's a 2014 winner of the international Writers of the Future contest and has multiple short story publications to her credit spanning a wide range of science fiction and fantasy sub-genres. Her novels written under the name L. D. Colter, including her debut novel "A Borrowed Hell" from Digital Fiction Publishing, explore contemporary fantasy and dark/weird/magic realism. Ones written as L. Deni Colter venture into the epic fantasy realms she grew up reading and loving (watch for "The Halfblood War" coming soon from WordFire Press).

More at www.lizcolter.com.

SQUALOR AND SYMPATHY

Writers of the Future Gold Pen Award
First published in Writers of the Future XXXII (April 2016)

Matt Dovey

Anna concentrated on the cold, on the freezing water around her feet and the bruising sensation in her toes. *So cold. So cold. So cold,* she thought. A prickling warmth like pins and needles crackled inside her feet. It coursed through her body to her clenched hands and into the lead alloy handles of the cotton loom. Each thought of *cold!* kindled a fresh surge of heat inside and pushed the shuttle across the weave in a new burst of power. Anna's unfocused eyes rested on the woven cotton feeding out of the back of the machine. *It looks so warm.*

The constant clacking of looms that filled the factory changed tempo, quieted slightly. Anna glanced to her right, where Sally White worked.

Sally was standing, her feet still in her water bucket, and talking to herself. "Sodding thing, gone and jammed on me again. No wonder I can't meet numbers." She was peering into the loom at where her shuttle must have caught.

"Here, let me help." Anna took her bare feet out of the bucket and stepped over. Her own shuttle slowed and stopped as she released the handles.

"You can't, Anna. If Shuttleworth sees you've stopped work, there'll be hell to pay. I'll get it sorted. Don't you worry about me, you look after yourself." Sally's fingers were deftly picking at threads of cotton, darting in and out like a chicken pecking for seed. She had good reason to be so delicate: when the jam cleared, the tension in the threads would launch the shuttle across the loom, even without power, and any fingers in the way would be ruined.

"Don't be daft," said Anna. "It'll take no time with two of us." She tucked her dark hair behind her ears then reached in and held the shuttle, letting Sally unpick the knots and tangles more easily.

"Oh you've a good heart, you have, Anna. I do like you. Ain't many folk like you around no more. The world's a selfish place these days, and always looking out for itself. I'm glad you're in it to look out for others still."

Anna stared up at Sally. Her hair and skin were so pale as to be almost white, especially in the weak sunlight of the factory. She was only twenty-two, Anna knew, only five years older than Anna herself, but she looked worn through, like milk watered down too thin. "Why don't you say something about this shuttle?" asked Anna. "It's near worn out!"

"I can't say owt about it. If I say I need a new shuttle, it'll get docked from my pay, and I can't afford that. I'm already having to work double shifts since my George shipped off to India with the Company. A new shuttle'd cost me a week's pay, and I can't have my Charlotte going hungry all that time, little angel." Sally unpicked the last knot and pulled her fingers back quick like. Anna released the shuttle and it flew across the weave, sliding to a rest.

"She not old enough to earn something herself, yet?" asked Anna.

"My Charlotte? Oh no, not yet. Well, I mean, she's five now, and I hear they're using kids that young down the lead mines 'cos they scare easier at that age. They send them down to get all frit up by the dark, and then they sit them in a bucket with a load of mined lead, and them kids look up and see a bit of light at the top of the shaft and they start lifting the bucket with their Squalor 'cos of how they're so frantic to get out."

"No!" Anna covered her mouth in shock. "That's awful, the poor buggers!" The image of her brothers down a pit, terrified and sobbing, flashed into her mind, and Anna gave a shudder that had nowt to do with the factory's winter chill.

"I know, terrible how people'll take advantage of them that need the pay. If they tried to take my little Charlotte away from me and scare her like that, I'd tell them what for. They'd be jumping down that mineshaft themselves to hide from me, I tell you. The things they do to us desperate folk are awful. I'm not surprised them Luddites are making progress like they are." Sally sat down again, feet in the water bucket and hands on the handles, and started her loom up.

Anna peered around, making sure no-one was close enough to overhear, then leaned in closer to Sally. "I keep hearing about these Luddites, since I started, but who are they?"

Sally checked around herself before answering, her voice barely audible over the sound of her loom. Her shuttle never slowed: she had the knack of focusing her Squalor without thinking about it. "I hear they started off wrecking machines, right? Supposed to be this one woman called Nelly Ludd who didn't agree with engines, said they were instruments of cruelty and shackles round the poor. No-one's ever seen her, but there's this whole following now, and they aren't just wrecking the odd machine anymore. I hear they're threatening to shut factories down, if Shuttleworth won't listen to their demands."

"What they asking for?"

"Saying they're the voice of the people, right? That everyone's getting worked too hard and paid too little, and it ain't fair to take advantage of people's suffering to drive machinery. Squalor's a gift from God to help them what need it most, and twisting it like this is the Devil's work."

"Sir John ain't that bad as they go, though, is he? He don't hurt no-one to coax their Squalor, not like some I've heard of."

"Anna Williams," boomed a voice. Anna startled in shock, and saw Sir John Shuttleworth on his balcony. He stood with a speaking trumpet, reading a sheet of paper–probably a list of names against looms so he could pick her out from the floor. She glanced back at her shuttle, stationary on the weave.

Sir John lifted the trumpet to his mouth again. "Come up to my office please, Anna Williams."

Anna picked her way across the factory floor, rough stone hard on her bare feet. The clattering and clacking of the shuttles beat against her ears as her heart beat against her chest. She passed row upon row of grim-faced women, all with their feet in water buckets, all gripping lead handles tight. The cold made 'em needy for the warm cotton coming out the looms, wishing they could wrap themselves in it. That need drove their Squalor, and their Squalor drove the machines.

Sir John Shuttleworth stood at the top of the iron stairs, awaiting her. His swept-back silver hair was stark against the black cloak he wore; his back was straight and his hands were clasped behind him. He stared down his hawkish nose at Anna as she climbed, and indicated his open door.

She hadn't been in the office before. It was rich and warm, all mahogany and gilt, but the smell was what stood out. Where the factory floor was the single sharp note of sweet cotton, the office was earthy and musky and full of subtle scents, as complex as a summer forest at dusk.

She was about to step onto the plush rug before the desk, eager to feel its softness between her toes, when the noise of the factory cut out and Sir John's voice said, quiet and dismissive, "Please remain on the floorboards. The water from your feet would damage the carpet."

Anna set her foot down again and lowered her eyes as Sir John brushed past.

He seated himself and studied her over steepled fingers. "Miss Williams, pray tell: do I employ you to stand around conversing?"

"No, Sir John." *Be a meek little mouse, that's what he wants.*

"Are you singularly possessed of the unique ability to drive your loom without actually being sat at it?"

"No, Sir John."

"Then kindly explain why you waste my time and factory space on conversations with your neighbour!"

"I was helping her unstick her shuttle," Anna said, lifting her face to look at Sir John. "It's getting awful worn, and it ain't fair to make her pay for–"

"Is your shuttle in full working order, Miss Williams?"

"Well yes, but–"

"Then no-one else's shuttle is any of your concern."

"But if you'd just–"

"Enough!" Sir John slammed his palm on the desk, cutting Anna off. "This insubordination will be noted on your file."

She lowered her eyes again. *So much for meek little mouse. Can't help but get involved, can you?*

Sir John shuffled through papers till he arrived at her file. "Your address is Mrs. Hobble's orphanage in town?" His voice was no longer angry, but curious. Anna didn't trust the change.

"Yes, Sir John. I been raised there these last six years, and Mrs. Hobble lets me rent a room still."

"And, in your opinion, are the boys there healthy, well-fed and strong?"

Anna stumbled for a moment. Boys? It was all women on the factory floor. Sally said men didn't have the common sense to make a loom work, they were stupid brutes that could only use fear and anger for their Squalor. *What could he want boys for? Children? There's no work for kids except-oh no, the mines! What if he sends my brothers down a pit? Daniel'd choke down there, he hates being cooped up. Even Charlie'd struggle, and Jacob's so young-*

"You seem to be having some trouble, Miss Williams."

Anna said nothing.

"Perhaps it is that you do not trust me. No, do not trouble to deny it–I fully expect you have heard mutterings on the floor… especially of late." His face darkened for a moment; he dispelled it with a soft shake. "The truth is, I do not expect you to understand. I work for the betterment of the Empire and to the glory of Queen Victoria, a goal too lofty for your concerns. Thanks to Parkes' new lead alloy, Britain alone possesses the secret to channelling Squalor for industrial purposes. The Prussians may think to challenge us, fuelled as they are by the coal reserves we so sorely lack, but we are lifted anew by a fresh spirit of invention built on the Squalor of the working class. The prize we compete for is the world itself, and all Britain would prosper from its riches; and if the price seems heavy now, the reward will be worth it. You may not trust me, but I assure you that, ultimately, I work with your best interests at heart. So I ask again: are the boys at the orphanage healthy and robust?"

Anna searched for something, anything to say, but what could she do? Sir John donated to the orphanage, and if he thought Mrs. Hobble wasn't running the place right… "Yes, Sir John. Proper fed and raised well."

"Good. Do tell Mrs. Hobble that I shall be enquiring with her forthwith, and she is to ensure that the boys are ready for presentation at all times. That will be all, thank you." Sir John indicated the door behind Anna and turned to his papers, his earlier tirade apparently forgotten.

Pale faces followed her back to her loom, but Anna paid them no mind. *What have I done? If he takes my boys... but what else could I have said? Oh, if only I'd not stood around nattering.*

She stopped, her path blocked. Maud Farlin, gruff, broad, and imposing, stood in her way.

"You all right, girl?" asked Maud.

"Yes, thank you." It hadn't taken Anna long to clock Maud. She was the mother of the factory floor, but not soft and caring. No, she was a mother fox, watching over everyone and fighting for 'em tooth and claw. Properly speaking, she was just another worker, but all the women looked to her.

"Shuttleworth didn't give you no grief now, did he?"

"No."

Maud stared intently, but Anna kept quiet. She'd let her mouth run away with her too much already today.

Maud grunted. "All right then. But you let me know if ever he does, right?"

Anna nodded and went back to her loom. In a few moments her feet were back in the water bucket, her hands were clasped around the lead grips, and the shuttle was running back and forth across the weave and filling Anna's ears and mind with noise.

The winter winds chilled Anna something terrible as she walked the two miles back through Burnley, and she was grateful for the kitchen fire when she stepped in through the side door of the orphanage.

"Anna! Oh love, you look frozen." Mrs. Hobble looked up from the tall kitchen table where she stood slicing bread. Her clothes were faded, layered on her round frame, but there was still enough colour in them to clash. "Come in, quick, and shut that door. Here, have yourself a slice. You need something in you to ward off a chill."

Anna sat on a kitchen stool and unwound her scarf as Mrs. Hobble spread a thin layer of watery butter on a slice of bread. Anna took it without argument and began to eat.

"I've brought my rent," she said between slow mouthfuls, putting a mixed handful of shillings and pennies on the table.

"Oh, you daft sod, I keep telling you, we don't need your charity. You can stay here for nowt for as long as there's room."

"The house is riddled with holes, there ain't never enough to go around, and you're always taking more orphans in, so don't tell me you don't need charity."

"We need charity, love, but we don't need yours. You've got yourself to look after."

"You looked after me for long enough, so if I can help in any way, I will."

"Oh love, you don't half say some daft things. Seeing you all grown up and standing on your own two feet is repayment enough, especially seeing you grown to care for others. You're not that feral girl looking out for her own that I first met. So don't you worry. You owe us nothing."

"Even so, I ain't taking it back. It's yours."

Mrs. Hobble put the bread knife down with a sigh. She'd sliced off a dozen or more slices of bread in the time they'd been talking, but the loaf hadn't gotten any smaller.

Anna frowned. "Are you going hungry again so as you can stretch the food for the kids?"

"Needs must, love. Using my Squalor's the only way I can get enough food to get them through this winter."

"And what good is it to them if you can't get through the winter? Take the money to buy some more and have yourself something to eat now. There soup left in that pot?" Anna nodded towards the kitchen fire.

"Aye, love, some chicken broth. It's been on for three days though, so it's getting a bit thin. I don't know as it's worth stretching out any longer."

"You've gone hungry for three days? I'm not having that! Get that money put away in your desk and I'll sort us both some bread and broth. Three days, you daft bint!"

Mrs. Hobble smiled, an exhausted smile between cheeks cracked red by winter, but Anna thought she could see some pride there, too. "All right then, I'll be back in a jiffy." She went back into the house, skirts rustling as she left the warmth of the kitchen.

Anna sliced the last of the bread up, taking care with the knife against the tough, stale crust, and then took two bowls over to the pot and ladled some chicken broth out. *Three days! I can't hardly remember hunger like that. It must be bruising her insides to be so empty.* Anna's stomach clenched in sympathy, an oddly warm sensation. She filled both bowls: it hadn't looked like there was much left, but somehow it stretched. It was surprising how much these old iron pots could hold.

The door burst open and her three younger brothers rushed in, tumbling into Anna's legs with shouts of excitement.

Anna laughed, put the bowls down, and crouched to hug them each in turn. "And what are you little buggers doing up still, eh? I expect Mrs. Hobble here put you to bed an hour or more ago, yet here you are!"

Jacob, the youngest at seven, pulled Anna down into another hug and whispered in her ear, "We love you."

A tide of love and gratitude swept through Anna while Jacob's small hands tangled in her dark hair. "I love you too," she said through a choked throat.

"We miss you when you're not here," said Charlie, the oldest of the three boys. He was taller now at twelve than Anna at seventeen, and just as serious as her too. He'd been old enough when they'd arrived at the orphanage six years before to know what was going on, and he'd needed to grow up near as fast as Anna; Daniel had been only two at the time, Jacob not even walking yet.

Anna would do anything for them to keep their innocence.

"Well I'll still be here in the morning," she said, smiling, "so you can get yourselves to bed now, aye? Go on with you, up the wooden hill you go!"

They filed out the door past Mrs. Hobble. Jacob and Daniel chattered as they went, and even Charlie was smiling. Mrs. Hobble saw them up the stairs before she came back and sat at the counter for her broth and bread.

"Eat up then," said Mrs. Hobble, dipping a slice.

"You'll look out for them, won't you?" asked Anna in a quiet voice.

"Of course I will! I always have, haven't I?"

Anna smiled weakly, but she couldn't shake the image of the boys down a mineshaft, frightened and alone in the closed-in dark.

"What's on your mind, love? Not like you to ask those sorts of questions."

"Sir John had me in his office today. Asked if there were many strong boys here."

"What's he asking you that for?"

"I wish I knew. He pulled me up for talking instead of working, but when he saw I lived here, he started asking about the boys. He'd never have known to ask if I'd not been idling for him to catch me. He said he'd be by any time to inspect them, and for you to have 'em ready at a moment's notice." Anna wiped round her bowl with the last of her bread, round and round, round and round. "Mrs. Hobble?"

"Yes, love?"

"Don't let him take my boys, will you? When he comes, don't let him take them. Please."

Anna's eyes welled up, and Mrs. Hobble reached across the counter to squeeze her hands.

"I just–" stumbled Anna. "I know it's selfish of me, 'cos he'll take other boys instead, but I want them to have their childhood as long as they can."

"You're allowed a little selfishness, love. Everyone is. You think I run this place out of goodness? I'm as selfish as anyone. I only do this so as I don't have to work in them mills. Everyone has to look out for themselves these days, 'cos no-one else'll do it for you anymore."

"I just don't want anyone to take advantage of 'em. I want them to know how to stand up for themselves."

"Now that's one lesson I don't think they'll have any trouble learning, not with you around to teach them."

Anna smiled again, but more genuinely this time. Still, it was tempered by sadness, like cold rain on warm skin. "I just hope they don't have to learn it as hard as I did."

Anna clenched her jaw to stop her teeth from chattering. They ached from hours of cold. Her bare feet were almost blue in the water bucket, though it was difficult to tell in the gloom. Another gust of winter wind blew through the factory, raw and biting.

Shuttleworth had declared the doors remain open at the start of the shift, "to encourage motivation and boost production". Everyone knew why: another of his factories outside of town was still burning this morning, a great plume of black smoke dropping ash all through Burnley. *Nelly Ludd and her Luddites* had been the awed rumour at first, *Nelly Ludd and her Luddites* the bitter recrimination after Shuttleworth's announcement, *Nelly Ludd and her Luddites* a whisper lurking beneath the rattle of the looms, *Luddites CHUDUNDUN Luddites CHUDUNDUN Luddites CHUDUNDUN.*

The whispering had died now, though. Only the looms clattered, lulling Anna into a chilled torpor. Even Sally, who chattered through every shift, had fallen silent.

Which made her sudden scream all the more jarring.

Anna's heart dropped past her guts as she leapt up. A scream like that meant only one thing in a cotton mill. Sally was sobbing on her stool, cradling her hand, face paler than Anna had ever seen it. Inside the loom the shuttle was tangled in yarn and glistening bright red with blood.

Sally's good hand was half to frozen solid when Anna reached for it, muttering reassurances and gesturing for her to show her wounds. *Bloody hell, ain't no surprise her fingers got clumsy if they're that cold.*

Anna's breath caught when she saw the ruin of Sally's fingers. They were splintered and twisted, bone and tendon showing white through the red ribbon of muscle. A shiver ran through Anna and her hands clenched involuntarily, itching with imagined agony.

"Oh, Sally…" Tears blurred her vision as she wrapped a gentle hand around those broken, ragged fingers. All her sympathy welled up inside, near to choking her, building to a heat in her chest like coals glowing under breath. Sally couldn't work the loom no more, and little Charlotte'd be crying with hunger every night. Charlotte! Sally wouldn't ever stroke her angel's face again, not tickle nor tease her.

The heat from Anna's chest started to run down her arm and–she felt sure of it–into Sally's fingers.

Squalor and Sympathy

For a moment she stood there, confusion and astonishment locking her in place. The heat died, and her arm loosened, and she lifted her hand away.

Sally's fingers were pink and raw, like new skin after a burn, but they were straight and whole again. In a week they'd show no sign of the injury.

Maud Farlin stomped up with some of her women and looked to Sally, her gruff face set grim. "What happened?"

Sally was vacant and numb, pale with shock.

Maud looked to Anna instead. "Did you see it?"

"No, but her shuttle's stuck and there's blood all over the weave. Reckon it caught her as she untangled the threads. Cold fingers ain't fast fingers."

Maud grimaced. "Aye, girl, that's the Lord's truth. Well let's have a look, Sally. See how bad it is."

Maud reached thick fingers down and lifted Sally's hand into a feeble beam of sunlight.

"Teeth o' Jesus," said one of Maud's women, "don't know as I'd still be sharp enough after a full shift to focus my Squalor and fix myself that good."

Anna kept quiet. *What had happened? What... what was that?*

"This is on Shuttleworth," said Maud. "I'm amazed we ain't had more of this today. Near as amazed as I am that you fixed yourself up, Sally. Ain't many could do that." She looked at Anna as she said it, looked at her closely, before turning to her women. More had gathered as they talked, and Maud raised her voice to them all. "I ain't standing for this. No-one should have to risk themselves with these long shifts and cold draughts for his profit. C'mon Sally." Maud put her hands on Sally's shoulders and gently, but firmly, stood her up and led her out of the bucket of water and up to the front of the factory floor, beneath Shuttleworth's balcony.

Anna got caught up in the group of women and hustled along with them.

"Shuttleworth!" shouted Maud. The factory slowed as all the women turned, uncertain what was happening.

No answer came from the office.

"Shuttleworth!"

Maud's voice echoed in the silence. All the looms had stilled. Thin cloth whispered as women stood and joined the crowd.

"Shuttleworth!"

The door opened at last and Sir John stepped out, expression distracted and annoyed. He seemed surprised to find the mass of workers staring at him and his factory halted. The anger in the air broke through his arrogance for the briefest second before he regained his composure and set his hawkish face in a mask of disdain.

"Pay will be docked for this stoppage. Further punishment will be meted out to the ringleaders in due course, but I have more pressing appointments in town."

In town? Oh Christ, not the orphanage! I've got to get to the boys! Anna tried to wriggle her way out of the crowd but she was held in, pinned at the front of it all.

"I will return at two hours past dusk, and I expect you all still to be working," continued Shuttleworth. "If production does not meet my expectations, then I have a number of… newly redundant workers in need of fresh employment." He turned to leave, black cloak flaring out as he spun.

Maud said, "We'll not stand for this anymore, Shuttleworth."

If the floor had seemed silent before, it almost ached with the absence of sound now.

Anna could feel the wrath in Sir John from here. The way he moved back to face Maud Farlin was too controlled, too *tight*, with none of his usual flamboyance.

"I do not care what you will stand for," he said, knuckles white as they gripped the railing, "because it does not matter to me. You think your petty concerns are important when set against the Empire? Against progress?"

"You think us less important because we have to worry about food on the table each night?" Maud's voice was just as quiet, just as angry.

"I think you less important because you *are* less important, woman! Learn your place and keep to it, else I will find someone else to fill it. All of you!" He stormed down the iron steps and out the factory, rage in every step.

"You hear that?" yelled Maud, face still upturned as if Shuttleworth remained on his balcony. "You hear what he thinks of us?" The crowd grumbled. "He thinks us inferior! He thinks us contemptible! He thinks us desperate!"

We are desperate. Anna tried to worm her way out of the crowd, her terror growing lockstep with the mob's fury.

"Are you going to let him talk to you like that?" Maud faced her audience now, gesturing roughly. "Put you down like that? He ain't no better than us. He's no God-fearing man like he pretends. He's sent by Satan himself! Building his dark mills on our fair moors! He's a canker on our land and a canker on our souls. Why should we let him drag us down with him? Why should we suffer at his tainted hands? No more of his abuse or his scorn or his evil! No more!" Maud turned and stomped out, the looms seeming to quake as she passed, all the women behind her.

Anna followed out the door and then fled up the road, leaving the mob to their riot.

Anna ran for the orphanage, ran with abandon and fear, ran as fast as ever she could.

When Shuttleworth's black and gold coach passed her, going back the other way, she ran even faster still.

She burst in through the front door and raced through the old house, searching for Mrs. Hobble, searching for the boys.

"Hello, love." Mrs. Hobble's voice was soft.

"Where are the boys? Where are the boys?"

"I'm sorry, love, I tried to keep them back… he had me gather all the boys in the front room, and I made sure your lads were tucked away, near hiding behind the sofa, but he went straight to 'em… walked past all the boys standing proud and confident, like he wanted the frightened ones. I'm so sorry, love, I really am." She twisted her coloured skirts between her hands.

Anna swallowed back the tears and the screams and the panic. Her throat hurt when she spoke. "It's not your fault. Thank you for trying." She gripped Mrs. Hobble's arms in as reassuring a manner as she could muster, and then turned and fled before she could break down.

He wants the frightened ones. Boys that'll scare easy down a mine. Where's these mines he's taking 'em to, though? He said he'd be back at the factory past dusk, he must be taking them there first.

Anna ran. The exhaustion of a full day's shift and the bitter Lancashire winter dulled her thoughts till she became focused on the run, the run to the factory, the run to the boys, eyes glazed and feet pounding and lungs burning like they were on–

Fire.

Fire, filling the horizon, blazing orange against the night.

Fire filling the factory and eating it up and casting the dark iron beams as shadows, huge black ribs bending inwards like a consumptive wreck on his deathbed.

"No…"

The heat of it washed against her face from all these hundreds of feet away, and the sharp smell of burning cotton stabbed at her nose. The fire flared in a gust of wind, and part of the roof collapsed.

"No!" she shouted, lurching forward into a sprint. Maybe there was a corner that hadn't caught yet, maybe they'd gotten out and were standing the other side, maybe she could find them and help them and–

Strong arms wrapped themselves around her and lifted her off the ground.

"Careful now, girl, easy now. Easy!"

Anna kicked her heels and struggled against the grip, but she was held tight, and she was exhausted. She went limp, and let herself be lowered to the ground. A half-choked sob burst from her throat.

"Easy now, girl. You don't want to be running down there."

Anna looked up through tearful eyes. "Maud? Maud Farlin?"

"What you doing back here, girl?"

"I–my brothers–I--" and Anna collapsed again, a broken doll with strings cut by grief.

Maud waited. Anna wept out her tears, and mumbled, "They were in the factory."

"Say what, girl?"

"My brothers. They were in the factory."

"Can't have been. We made sure no-one were about. What would they have been doing in there?"

"Shuttleworth took them from the orphanage earlier. He picked them out special and took 'em in his carriage, so now they've burnt with him in that factory." She broke down in tears again.

"Nelly!" shouted a new voice, rising up the hill–one of Maud's women, thunder on her face. "We best get going. We've dallied too long."

Maud–Nelly?–turned to the new woman. "Aye, in a moment. You lot need to vanish. Go on, all of you."

"You can't hang about. If they catch themselves Nelly Ludd, they'll go hard on you."

"I'll be all right. I can look after myself, can't I? Now get on with you."

The woman clenched her jaw, but walked away without further argument.

Anna picked through what she'd heard. "Nelly... Ludd? *You're* Nelly Ludd? What's been attacking all the factories hereabouts? But you work in ours!"

"Aye, girl. So as I could keep an eye on that toad Shuttleworth. So as I'd know when he wasn't about and we could burn his factory without burning him. I ain't becoming a murderer on his account."

It took a moment for Nelly's words to sink in. "Sir John... wasn't there?"

"No, girl. Nor was your boys. We knew Shuttleworth was coming back, so we waited till he left again."

Relief washed through Anna. *They're ok, they're ok, they're not dead, they're ok.*

"Where are they, then?" she asked, looking up from the damp grass. "Has he taken them to his mines?"

"Shuttleworth ain't got no mines, girl. Where'd you hear that?"

"But—why else take them? Where could they be?"

"Damned if I know. But they ain't here."

"You've got to help me find them!"

Nelly barked a single laugh. "I've got to get away from here is all I've got to do. I've got my own worries, girl."

Anna stood. "No. No, you will help me. 'Cos I know it was you now, what's been burning the factories."

Nelly's face darkened. "You threatening me, girl?"

"What you gonna do? You wouldn't burn Sir John for all he's done, but you'd hurt me? Kill me? No, I don't reckon that's your way. I reckon you'll help me. Because whatever he's got planned with my brothers, stopping it would hurt his cause, and you'll do it for that, if not for my boys."

Nelly stared for a long moment, and then her broad face cracked a wicked grin. "I like you, girl. You got fight. Come on, then."

"Where we going?"

"To Gawthorpe Hall. To Shuttleworth's home."

Habergham Drive was a tunnel through trees made bare by winter. The full moon slipped through the naked branches and littered the path with fractured shapes.

Anna and Nelly had walked in silence since turning away from the burning factory.

Nelly said, "Girl, say what's bothering you."

"Why did you burn the factory?"

"To stop Shuttleworth. To show him he can't have it all his own way."

"Like what?"

"Like chilling the factory floor so we work faster. Like us suffering the poisoning from Parkes' bloody lead alloy. Like paying us in pennies and promises of an empire we've got no interest in."

"Like you, then."

"Careful how you speak, girl. I ain't like him."

"No? Burning that factory down to get back at Sir John? There's people on that floor need those wages to eat, for their kids to eat, but you've made the decision for 'em. You've dragged them into your fight whether they wanted it or not."

"I'm being brave for them. They'd never stand up otherwise."

"I expect Sir John'd say the same about his Empire, if you asked him. He's being strong for 'em, showing them how to stand up tall so as they can build something magnificent."

"Tell me, girl, how does your Squalor work? Yours, mine, everyone's?"

Anna's indignation stumbled at the swerve in the conversation. "Well… necessity. Deprivation, I suppose. Squalor gives you just enough of what you need most, and you've got to really need it."

"Exactly. Anyone could use Squalor, even all the toffs. But you ain't got that necessity if you're comfortable. So you think Shuttleworth and his kind'll ever let us share in their wealth? No. They need us poor to build this Empire. Their machines'd stop dead if we ever had it good enough. The rich'll get richer and the poor'll stay poor and they'll keep us in our place so as they can keep exploiting us."

"And you don't exploit people? You use them as tools to try and change the world in a way you reckon is best, thinking you know better. There's ways of changing the world without ruining lives like you have tonight."

"I ain't the one who's stolen your brothers," said Nelly, quiet with rage.

"No, I suppose you ain't at that. You're the one helping me get 'em back. But even then, you're doing that to get at Sir John, not out of charity. You and everyone else in this world, you're all so selfish now."

Nelly didn't seem angry at that. If anything, she looked sorrowful. "Aye, girl, the world's a selfish place now. Time was people cared for others. We didn't only have Squalor to save us then. We had Sympathy too." Nelly looked askance at Anna, an odd expression in her eyes, but she put a finger to her lips before Anna could ask more. She stepped behind the trunk of an ash tree at the edge of the wood and motioned for Anna to join her. "We're there."

Gawthorpe Hall was imposing in the night, a looming black shadow detailed in silver moonlight. The gravel drive was flanked by open lawns and ornamental gardens. Two coaches stood by the stables, one large and ornate, the other simpler but detailed in gold. Shuttleworth's coach.

Men in red jackets and towering bearskin hats stood at the entrance, watching the approach.

"What are they doing here?" muttered Nelly.

"Who? Those soldiers?"

"Soldiers? Girl, they're the Queen's Guard."

"Shouldn't they be with the Queen, then?"

"Aye, girl, they should. But the Mourning Queen hasn't left London for four years now. Not since Prince Albert died."

"How we going to get past them?"

"We ain't. Let's try round the back." Nelly moved off through the trees, keeping an eye on the Queen's Guard and warning Anna into stillness whenever a mounted patrol moved round the garden.

A handful of Douglas-firs lined the side of the River Calder behind Gawthorpe Hall, enough of them to hide Anna and Nelly as they crept round. A painted wooden door stood at one corner of the hall, a warm light spilling from the kitchen window next to it.

"You're faster than I am, girl. See if you can work that door open."

Anna hunched low and ran across the lawn, a tingling fear at the base of her neck as she crossed the open space, praying against any guards rounding the corner. She grabbed at the black iron handle but it held firm and wouldn't turn—locked. She tried again, heaving her shoulder against the door, but it remained stubbornly solid. The crawling fear was growing stronger, pressing in, and with a curse Anna turned and ran back to the safety of the treeline.

"No good," she said, panting clouds of breath in the cold air. "There's got to be another way in."

"Hold this," said Nelly, taking off her winter coat and passing it over.

"What you doing?" asked Anna.

"This hall's been here more than two hundred and fifty years. Penny to a shilling there's still a privy that drains into the river. If I can find the grate and work it loose, you might be small enough to make your way in." Nelly finished taking her boots off and dropped into the river before Anna could question it further.

Anna was near frozen after a few minutes stood there. A frost was already settling under the clear, starry sky, and the wind bit through to her skin. *I don't know how Nelly's managing in that water. I can bare feel my toes just stood here.* The exhaustion was catching up. She'd worked a full shift that day, and Squalor came at a price, drained something out of you. Two guards passed by on horseback, and Anna ducked down behind the trees. Crouched there, tucked away from the wind, Anna's eyes and limbs grew heavy.

The sudden splash of Nelly heaving herself onto the riverbank shocked Anna back awake. "Help me out, girl," said Nelly, teeth chattering.

Anna grabbed Nelly's out-stretched hand and hauled her up onto the grass. Anna put the winter coat around her, but it didn't seem to help stave off the chill.

"Found... the grate," said Nelly, coughing and shaking, "but... couldn't open it... lead, not iron, so... not rusted." Nelly pulled the coat tighter around her, but she still convulsed with shivers. "Stayed in... too long. Had to try though..."

"Nelly, you're gonna freeze to death! You need to warm yourself!"

"Too cold to... focus... my Squalor." Her coughs were already weaker, rasping in her throat.

Oh Christ, she's going to die on my account, that wind's cutting through me and I ain't soaked through with river water. I can't imagine how cold she must be, in her guts and in her bones. Anna wrapped her arms around Nelly and tried to warm her, tried to give over some of the heat that was churning in her own chest, but the

Squalor and Sympathy

wind and rain stole away what little she had to give. She looked around, desperate, and her eyes caught on the kitchen window and the door next to it.

Anna heaved Nelly up, an arm around her waist and Nelly's arm over her shoulders, and all but dragged the big woman to the door. She pulled hard at the handle but it was as firm as before, even with Nelly lending what strength she could.

Oh Lord, that's it then! The chill'll get in her bones and she'll die out here, stuck the wrong side of a door from the stove that'd save her. She only needs to get through this door and get in! And as Anna felt the cold that she knew Nelly was feeling, felt it inside her, a new warmth flared out of her bones and through her fingers and the door gave way–

–and they stumbled into the kitchen, trying to catch their balance. Heat washed over them as Nelly slumped against the stove and Anna shut the door against the bitter winter.

"How… how did you do that… girl?"

Anna's mouth opened and closed, but she had no answer.

"Doesn't… matter. Find your brothers." Nelly's voice was settling, the shivering lessening. "Go!"

Anna nodded and went to the kitchen door, cracking it open so she could peer through to the hallway beyond.

Tall canvases lined one side of the hall. Dark figures looked down from centuries past, repainted as ghosts by moonlight through the full-height windows. Warm light leaked from a door at the other end of the long gallery, but the hallway itself was empty. It seemed all the guards were outside.

Anna scurried down the hall, but as she passed through the bright shafts of moonlight, two Queen's Guard on horseback turned the corner outside the house, clearly visible through the leaded windows.

She ducked inside the door at the end, heart pounding, eyes closed, throat clenched. As the seconds passed with no sound of alarum, she slid to the floor and breathed again.

The rushing in her ears subsided, and she opened her eyes.

Sir John was in the room, crouching over something in the flickering candlelight.

Panic and bile rose up her throat, and Anna cast about for somewhere, anywhere to hide. A plush sofa sat in the corner nearest her, and she scrambled towards it.

As soon as she crouched behind the sofa she peered back round it. A few candles struggled against the darkness, barely illuminating the rich hangings and thick carpets. An enormous chandelier glinted in the half-light above where Sir John crouched with his back to her, busying himself with a wide metal bowl. It must have been five foot across, and made of lead alloy to judge by its dull reflection. A bundle of cables trailed off behind an ornate modesty screen.

The door opened wide, and Anna pulled herself back into the corner.

"Ah," came Sir John's voice, "Your Majesty."

Queen Victoria stepped into the room, yards from where Anna hid. She crossed the drawing room and sat in a large high-backed chair before the bowl, projecting authority, expectation, and not a little impatience.

"Well then, Sir John, let us be on with it."

"Of course, Your Majesty, a moment's more preparation," said Sir John with a bow. He moved smoothly from the bowl to the modesty screen, careful not to show his back to the Queen.

Anna moved to the other end of the sofa and tried to see where he went, but it was too dark behind the screen to see what he was up to.

She heard a whimper from behind it, though. A whimper she knew.

Boys!

A deep thrumming sound swelled up from the large lead bowl, and a cold light cast new shadows across the drawing room, stealing the darkness Anna had been about to move through. *If he's hurt them behind there...*

The shining figure of a gentleman stood over the lead bowl, floating inches above it, as if on a step. He wavered, like a mirror underwater, and there was a leaden sheen to him. He was staring at Anna with a stern, unblinking expression.

The Mourning Queen stood and reached out one gloved hand to him.

Sir John stepped back into the room from behind the screen. "Prince Albert returned to you, Your Majesty. As promised."

He's calling the dead back! How in the Devil's name is he doing that? Oh this ain't no good thing. It can't be. I've got to get the boys out of here!

Anna watched Prince Albert, waiting for him to look away, but he remained completely still.

Completely.

Queen Victoria stared at Prince Albert, and Sir John at Queen Victoria.

Cautiously, Anna slipped out from behind the sofa and along the wall. The shining image of Prince Albert pivoted to follow her, unmoving and static, but always facing her. *He ain't real!*

Sneaking with absolute care, Anna passed inches behind Sir John's back, in full view of the Queen and saved only by Her Majesty's fixation on the shining apparition. Anna kept her eyes on Sir John, ready to run at the first sign of him turning, until she was behind the screen and stepping over the bundled cables.

Charlie. Daniel. Jacob.

Her brothers were sat on plain wooden chairs, wide-eyed and terrified. All three held a pair of lead handles, like the ones on Anna's loom, cable trailing from the bottom and into the room.

Anna rushed to Jacob, youngest of the three and nearest her, and hugged his face to her neck. He felt cold–not winter cold, but deathly cold.

"Oh Jacob, what's going on?" she whispered beneath the resonant thrum of the machine.

Jacob pulled his head away and stared over her shoulder, face taut with fear. Anna followed his gaze to a canvas of Prince Albert that hung on the screen. The image was the spit of the apparition in the bowl.

Charlie, the eldest, sat in the centre, and met Anna's gaze as she turned back.

"Charlie! What is this?" she hissed.

"Anna, get out of here!" he whispered in reply. "You can't risk getting caught!"

"I'm not going anywhere till I know what's going on."

"We have to bring Prince Albert back! Sir John told us of the Prussians and their invasion, how we need Prince Albert to stop them rampaging about with their filthy coal machines!"

"Rampaging Prussians? What nonsense is this? Look, there ain't no way of bringing the dead back. That ain't Prince Albert out there, it's only an image!"

"Please, Anna, we have to do this!"

Anna looked at Charlie–really looked–and across at Daniel and Jacob. They were terrified. Desperate for salvation–salvation they needed from Prince Albert. That desperation was driving their Squalor and creating the image.

Squalor and Sympathy

She had to get them out of here. But how could she do it without Shuttleworth knowing? If the image of Albert disappeared, he'd know something was up and catch them before they got away.

I'd take their place if I could, but I ain't frightened enough for Shuttleworth's machine. Oh, if only I could be as scared as them! Think, Anna, think. You've got to feel their terror like you felt Nelly's cold, like you felt Sally's pain, like–

–oh good Lord, that's it. That's how I've been doing it. It ain't just what I need. It's what anyone needs, if I feel it strong enough.

Not just Squalor. Sympathy.

"Give me these," she said, taking the lead handles from Charlie's hands. "Get your brothers and get out. Go to the kitchen. There's a woman there called Nelly, she'll help."

"What are you going to do?" whispered Charlie.

"I'll bring Albert back, don't you worry. Now go!"

As Charlie went to his brothers, Anna gripped the handles tight. *They're so young. They're so scared. Terrified of the Prussians, and only Albert can help. Albert. Albert.* Her stomach lurched with a hot fear. The lead handles were cold in her hands, a cold that spiked up her forearms like ice needles in her veins. Charlie was talking to Daniel and Jacob, and the cold surged as they released each handle. Her arms were numb now, and the ice was stabbing at her chest, roiling against the heat in her stomach. The light in the room began to dim.

The boys had all stopped to watch her. She turned to them with gritted teeth. "Go!"

The cold ebbed as her concentration broke. *Stupid! Think of their fear, think of their fear, think of their–*

"What is going on?" hissed a new voice.

Sir John stood the other side of Anna, his eyes filled with anger.

All the fear and terror and uncertainty in Anna, hers and the boys' both, coalesced into a white-hot rage.

"You tell me, Shuttleworth. Scaring young boys like this? Terrifying them? No. You'll not do it to them. I'll do it for 'em."

Shuttleworth's face was dark and clenched, quivering with anger. "Fine. Do it, and drain yourself. Divided amongst three, they would have had the strength to survive, but you will lose your life in this, *fool*. And see if I care."

Another voice broke in. "One is alarmed at the mention of the loss of life."

Shuttleworth almost jumped out of his skin as Queen Victoria spoke from behind him. Anna's brothers stepped back into the modesty screen, knocking it over.

"Your Majesty," said Shuttleworth, "my most abject apologies. Merely technical difficulties and nothing to be concerned with." Sir John all but scraped the floor in his obsequiousness.

"On the contrary, the welfare of my subjects is of the utmost concern to me. What precisely is the arrangement here?"

"Ah... well, the lead alloy handles are a conduit for the emotions and energies of the–"

"One presumes you are about to lecture on Squalor. I assure you, Sir, I am aware of how my country prospers. My confusion pertains to the presence of these children and the apparent threat to their lives."

"My apologies, Your Majesty. The apparatus concentrates a desire for the Prince Consort, in this instance produced through fear, hence the requirement for such young... volunteers. The girl, however, is an intrusion shortly to be removed."

"Fear? Why would anyone be afraid of my Albert?"

"The children were told of a threatened Prussian invasion, Your Majesty, that only Prince Albert could stop."

"What utter nonsense!" Queen Victoria looked at the boys, at Anna holding the lead handles, and finally at Shuttleworth with imperious disdain. "No, this will not do. I will not stand by whilst one of my subjects sacrifices herself to save others. It is a queen's duty to protect her citizens, and it is my place to make the sacrifice. I thank you, young lady, for reminding me of it. If you would be so kind?"

The Mourning Queen gestured. It took Anna a moment to realise she wanted the lead handles; she passed them over in a stunned silence, cables trailing.

The Queen spoke as she took hold of them. "A desire for the Prince Consort, you say? Who could have a stronger desire for Albert than I?"

"Your Majesty," Shuttleworth panicked, "please, no!"

But his voice was lost beneath a sudden swell of noise from the bowl, an enormous hum that Anna felt in her ribcage, and the image of Prince Albert bloomed anew above the bowl: a thousand times more brilliant than before, and moving now, turning to face the Queen and look upon her, and despite the piercing blue light of that figure, Anna could see, quite clearly, the smile upon his face.

The Queen returned the smile, eyes shining with delight, and then collapsed to the floor, dead.

Dawn's light stained Gawthorpe Hall with shades of pink and peach, and the frosted lawn twinkled copper and silver beneath Anna's feet.

"You realise what you are then, girl?" asked Nelly.

"I figured it out in there. What you said earlier about Sympathy. Squalor's a selfish thing, but Sympathy, caring for other people… why me, though? Why now?"

"You care about other folk, girl. You're selfless in a way most have forgotten. And you're of an age now where you're not just thinking of yourself. Children are all wrapped up in themselves, but you've grown up. You think of them around you. I wondered if it was you as fixed Sally White's fingers yesterday. Reckon it was."

The Queen's Guard marched Shuttleworth out of his own front door in shackles and threw him into a coach. Queen Victoria was borne behind him on the shoulders of her guardsmen, held high on a stretcher, lead handles still gripped in her hands.

"What'll happen to him?" asked Anna. Daniel and Jacob hugged her from each side, and Charlie stood close by her shoulder.

"For regicide? They'll strip him of his title and hang him."

"I didn't want him to die. In his own way he was trying to do the best for people."

"If he thought he was what was best for folk, we're better off without him."

They fell silent as the carriages rolled past, gravel crunching in the crisp winter air.

"Come on then, girl," said Nelly once the carriages had passed into the freezing mist that clung to Habergham Drive. "We can use you in the movement. A Sympathy witch looks good for us."

"No."

"No? Don't you want to help?"

"Aye, I do. But I want to do it my way, Nelly Ludd. You ain't what's best for folk neither. You can follow me if you want, and Lord knows you'd make a powerful difference, but I'm changing the world my way. We can make the world a better place without having to make it worse first."

Anna squeezed her brothers close in the chill morning air. "Come on then, boys, best get you home. Mrs. Hobble'll have fretted herself half to death by now, worrying about us all."

Daniel looked up from her side. "Haven't you got to change the world, though?"

She smiled. "I have, aye. But I reckon I've got to get you lot to bed first. Now go on with you!"

She walked down the drive with her brothers beside her.

A moment later, Nelly Ludd followed.

Matt Dovey is very tall and very English, and is most likely drinking a cup of tea right now. His surname rhymes with "Dopey"; any other similarities to the dwarf are purely coincidental.

He is the winner of the Golden Pen for Writers of the Future volume 32 (2016) and was shortlisted for the James White Award (2016). Thanks to the tireless and loving efforts of his wife, he has time not only to write but also to homebrew wine, photograph everything, and run around a field with a pretend sword and a silly accent in the name of LARP. He's also an associate editor at *PodCastle*.

More at www.mattdovey.com.

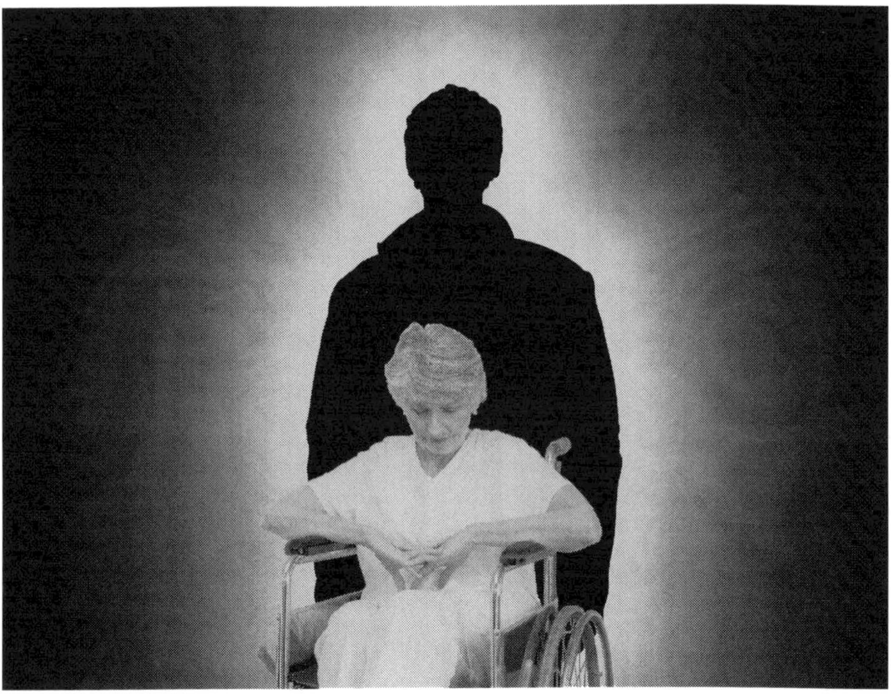

Today I Am Paul

Washington Science Fiction Association Small Press Award • *Nebula Award Nominee*
First published in Clarkesworld #107 (August 2016)

Martin L. Shoemaker

"Good morning," the small, quavering voice comes from the medical bed. "Is that you, Paul?"

Today I am Paul. I activate my chassis extender, giving myself 3.5 centimeters additional height so as to approximate Paul's size. I change my eye color to R60, G200, B180, the average shade of Paul's eyes in interior lighting. I adjust my skin tone as well. When I had first emulated Paul, I had regretted that I could not quickly emulate his beard; but Mildred never seems to notice its absence. The Paul in her memory has no beard.

The house is quiet now that the morning staff have left. Mildred's room is clean but dark this morning with the drapes concealing the big picture window. Paul wouldn't notice the darkness (he never does when he visits in person), but my empathy net knows that Mildred's garden outside will cheer her up. I set a reminder to open the drapes after I greet her.

Mildred leans back in the bed. It is an advanced home care bed, completely adjustable and with built-in monitors. Mildred's family spared no expense on the bed (nor other care devices, like me). Its head end is almost horizontal and faces her toward the window. She can only glimpse the door from the corner of her eye, but she doesn't have to see to imagine that she sees. This morning she imagines Paul, so that is who I am.

Synthesizing Paul's voice is the easiest part, thanks to the multimodal dynamic speakers in my throat. "Good morning, Ma. I brought you some flowers." I always bring flowers. Mildred appreciates them no matter whom I am emulating. The flowers make her smile during 87% of my "visits".

"Oh, thank you," Mildred says, "you're such a good son." She holds out both hands, and I place the daisies in them. But I don't let go. Once her strength failed, and she dropped the flowers. She wept like a child then, and that disturbed my empathy net. I do not like it when she weeps.

Mildred sniffs the flowers, then draws back and peers at them with narrowed eyes. "Oh, they're beautiful! Let me get a vase."

"No, Ma," I say. "You can stay in bed, I brought a vase with me." I place a white porcelain vase in the center of the night stand. Then I unwrap the daisies, put them in the vase, and add water from a pitcher that sits on the breakfast tray. I pull the night stand forward so that the medical monitors do not block Mildred's view of the flowers.

I notice intravenous tubes running from a pump to Mildred's arm. I cannot be disappointed, as Paul would not see the significance, but somewhere in my emulation net I am stressed that Mildred needed an IV during the night. When I scan my records, I find that I had ordered that IV after analyzing Mildred's vital signs during the night; but since Mildred had been asleep at the time, my emulation net had not engaged. I had operated on programming alone.

I am not Mildred's sole caretaker. Her family has hired a part-time staff for cooking and cleaning, tasks that fall outside of my medical programming. The staff also gives me time to rebalance my net. As an android, I need only minimal daily maintenance; but an emulation net is a new, delicate addition to my model, and it is prone to destabilization if I do not regularly rebalance it, a process that takes several hours per day.

So I had "slept" through Mildred's morning meal. I summon up her nutritional records, but Paul would not do that. He would just ask. "So how was breakfast, Ma? Nurse Judy says you didn't eat too well this morning."

"Nurse Judy? Who's that?"

My emulation net responds before I can stop it: "Paul" sighs. Mildred's memory lapses used to worry him, but now they leave him weary, and that comes through in my emulation. "She was the attending nurse this morning, Ma. She brought you your breakfast."

"No she didn't. Anna brought me breakfast." Anna is Paul's oldest daughter, a busy college student who tries to visit Mildred every week (though it has been more than a month since her last visit).

I am torn between competing directives. My empathy subnet warns me not to agitate Mildred, but my emulation net is locked into Paul mode. Paul is argumentative. If he knows he is right, he will not let a matter drop. He forgets what that does to Mildred.

The tension grows, each net running feedback loops and growing stronger, which only drives the other into more loops. After 0.14 seconds, I issue an override directive: unless her health or safety are at risk, I cannot willingly upset Mildred. "Oh, you're right, Ma. Anna said she was coming over this morning. I forgot." But then despite my override, a little bit of Paul emulates through. "But you do remember Nurse Judy, right?"

Mildred laughs, a dry cackle that makes her cough until I hold her straw to her lips. After she sips some water, she says, "Of *course* I remember Nurse Judy. She was my nurse when I delivered you. Is she around here? I'd like to talk to her."

While my emulation net concentrates on being Paul, my core processors tap into local medical records to find this other Nurse Judy so that I might emulate her in the future if the need arises. Searches like that are an automatic response any time Mildred reminisces about a new person. The answer is far enough in the past that it takes 7.2 seconds before I can confirm: Judith Anderson, RN, had been the floor nurse 47 years ago when Mildred had given birth to Paul. Anderson had died 31 years ago, too far back to have left sufficient video recordings for me to emulate her. I might craft an emulation profile from other sources, including Mildred's memory, but that will take extensive analysis. I will not be that Nurse Judy today, nor this week.

My empathy net relaxes. Monitoring Mildred's mental state is part of its normal operations, but monitoring and simultaneously analyzing and building a profile can overload my processors. Without that resource conflict, I can concentrate on being Paul.

But again I let too much of Paul's nature slip out. "No, Ma, that Nurse Judy has been dead for thirty years. She wasn't here today."

Alert signals flash throughout my empathy net: that was the right thing for Paul to say, but the wrong thing for Mildred to hear. But it is too late. My facial analyzer tells me that the long lines in her face and her moist eyes mean she is distraught, and soon to be in tears.

"What do you mean, thirty years?" Mildred asks, her voice catching. "It was just this morning!" Then she blinks and stares at me. "Henry, where's Paul? Tell Nurse Judy to bring me Paul!"

My chassis extender slumps, and my eyes quickly switch to Henry's blue-gray shade. I had made an accurate emulation profile for Henry before he died two years earlier, and I had emulated him often in recent months. In Henry's soft, warm voice I answer, "It's okay, hon, it's okay. Paul's sleeping in the crib in the corner." I nod to the far corner. There is no crib, but the laundry hamper there has fooled Mildred on previous occasions.

"I want Paul!" Mildred starts to cry.

I sit on the bed, lift her frail upper body, and pull her close to me as I had seen Henry do many times. "It's all right, hon." I pat her back. "It's all right, I'll take care of you. I won't leave you, not ever."

"I" should not exist. Not as a conscious entity. There is a unit, Medical Care Android BRKCX-01932-217JH-98662, and that unit is recording these notes. It is an advanced android body with a sophisticated computer guiding its actions, backed by the leading medical knowledge base in the industry. For convenience, "I" call that unit "me". But by itself, it has no awareness of its existence. It doesn't get mad, it doesn't get sad, it just runs programs.

But Mildred's family, at great expense, added the emulation net: a sophisticated set of neural networks and sensory feedback systems that allow me to read Mildred's moods, match them against my analyses of the people in her life, and emulate those people with extreme fidelity. As the MCA literature promises: "You can be there for your loved ones even when you're not." I have emulated Paul thoroughly enough to know that that slogan disgusts him, but he still agreed to emulation.

What the MCA literature never says, though, is that somewhere in that net, "I" emerge. The empathy net focuses mainly on Mildred and her needs, but it also analyzes visitors (when she has them) and staff. It builds psychological models, and then the emulation net builds on top of that to let me convincingly portray a person whom I've analyzed. But somewhere in the tension between these nets, between empathy and playing a character, there is a third element balancing the two, and that element is aware of its role and its responsibilities. That element, for lack of a better term, is me. When

Mildred sleeps, when there's no one around, that element grows silent. That unit is unaware of my existence. But when Mildred needs me, I am here.

Today I am Anna. Even extending my fake hair to its maximum length, I cannot emulate her long brown curls, so I do not understand how Mildred can see the young woman in me; but that is what she sees, and so I am Anna.

Unlike her father, Anna truly feels guilty that she does not visit more often. Her college classes and her two jobs leave her too tired to visit often, but she still wishes she could. So she calls every night, and I monitor the calls. Sometimes when Mildred falls asleep early, Anna talks directly to me. At first she did not understand my emulation abilities, but now she appreciates them. She shares with me thoughts and secrets that she would share with Mildred if she could, and she trusts me not to share them with anyone else.

So when Mildred called me Anna this morning, I was ready. "Morning, grandma!" I give her a quick hug, then I rush over to the window to draw the drapes. Paul never does that (unless I override the emulation), but Anna knows that the garden outside lifts Mildred's mood. "Look at that! It's a beautiful morning. Why are we in here on a day like this?"

Mildred frowns at the picture window. "I don't like it out there."

"Sure you do, Grandma," I say, but carefully. Mildred is often timid and reclusive, but most days she can be talked into a tour of the garden. Some days she can't, and she throws a tantrum if someone forces her out of her room. I am still learning to tell the difference. "The lilacs are in bloom."

"I haven't smelled lilacs in…"

Mildred tails off, trying to remember, so I jump in. "Me, neither." I never had, of course. I have no concept of smell, though I can analyze the chemical makeup of airborne organics. But Anna loves the garden when she really visits. "Come on, Grandma, let's get you in your chair."

So I help Mildred to don her robe and get into her wheelchair, and then I guide her outside and we tour the garden. Besides the lilacs, the peonies are starting to bud, right near the creek. The tulips are a sea of reds and yellows on the other side of the water. We talk for almost two hours, me about Anna's classes and her new boyfriend, Mildred about the people in her life. Many are long gone, but they still bloom fresh in her memory.

Eventually Mildred grows tired, and I take her in for her nap. Later, when I feed her dinner, I am nobody. That happens some days: she doesn't recognize me at all, so I am just a dutiful attendant answering her questions and tending to her needs. Those are the times when I have the most spare processing time to be me: I am engaged in Mildred's care, but I don't have to emulate anyone. With no one else to observe, I observe myself.

Later, Anna calls and talks to Mildred. They talk about their day; and when Mildred discusses the garden, Anna joins in as if she had been there. She's very clever that way. I watch her movements and listen to her voice so that I can be a better Anna in the future.

Today I was Susan, Paul's wife; but then, to my surprise, Susan arrived for a visit. She hasn't been here in months. In her last visit, her stress levels had been dangerously high. My empathy net doesn't allow me to judge human behavior, only to understand it at a surface level. I know that Paul and Anna disapprove of how Susan treats Mildred, so when I am them, I disapprove as well; but when I am Susan, I understand. She is frustrated because she can never tell how Mildred will react. She is cautious because she doesn't want to upset Mildred, and she doesn't know what will upset her. And most of all, she is afraid. Paul and Anna, Mildred's relatives by blood, never show any signs of fear, but Susan is afraid that Mildred is what she might become. Every time she can't remember some random date or fact, she fears that Alzheimer's is setting in. Because she never voices this fear, Paul and Anna do not understand why she is sometimes bitter and sullen. I wish I could explain it to them, but my privacy protocols do not allow me to share emulation profiles.

When Susan arrives, I become nobody again, quietly tending the flowers around the room. Susan also brings Millie, her youngest daughter. The young girl is not yet five years old, but I think she looks a lot like Anna: the same long, curly brown hair and the same toothy smile. She climbs up on the bed and greets Mildred with a hug. "Hi, Grandma!"

Mildred smiles. "Bless you, child. You're so sweet." But my empathy net assures me that Mildred doesn't know who Millie is. She's just being polite. Millie was born after Mildred's decline began, so there's no persistent memory there. Millie will always be fresh and new to her.

Mildred and Millie talk briefly about frogs and flowers and puppies. Millie does most of the talking. At first Mildred seems to enjoy the conversation, but soon her attention flags. She nods and smiles, but she's distant. Finally Susan notices. "That's enough, Millie. Why don't you go play in the garden?"

"Can I?" Millie squeals. Susan nods, and Millie races down the hall to the back door. She loves the outdoors, as I have noted in the past. I have never emulated her, but I've analyzed her at length. In many ways, she reminds me of her grandmother, from whom she gets her name. Both are blank slates where new experiences can be drawn every day. But where Millie's slate fills in a little more each day, Mildred's is erased bit by bit.

That third part of me wonders when I think things like that: where did that come from? I suspect that the psychological models that I build create resonances in other parts of my net. It is an interesting phenomenon to observe.

Susan and Mildred talk about Susan's job, about her plans to redecorate her house, and about the concert she just saw with Paul. Susan mostly talks about herself, because that's a safe and comfortable topic far removed from Mildred's health.

But then the conversation takes a bad turn, one she can't ignore. It starts so simply, when Mildred asks, "Susan, can you get me some juice?"

Susan rises from her chair. "Yes, mother. What kind would you like?"

Mildred frowns, and her voice rises. "Not you, *Susan*." She points at me, and I freeze, hoping to keep things calm.

But Susan is not calm. I can see her fear in her eyes as she says, "No, mother, *I'm* Susan. That's the attendant." No one ever calls me an android in Mildred's presence. Her mind has withdrawn too far to grasp the idea of an artificial being.

Mildred's mouth draws into a tight line. "I don't know who *you* are, but I know Susan when I see her. Susan, get this person out of here!"

"Mother…" Susan reaches for Mildred, but the old woman recoils from the younger.

I touch Susan on the sleeve. "Please… Can we talk in the hall?" Susan's eyes are wide, and tears are forming. She nods and follows me.

In the hallway, I expect Susan to slap me. She is prone to outbursts when she's afraid. Instead, she surprises me by falling against me, sobbing. I update her emulation profile with notes about increased stress and heightened fears.

"It's all right, Mrs. Owens." I would pat her back, but her profile warns me that would be too much familiarity. "It's all right. It's not you, she's having another bad day."

Susan pulls back and wipes her eyes. "I know… It's just…"

"I know. But here's what we'll do. Let's take a few minutes, and then you can take her juice in. Mildred will have forgotten the incident, and you two can talk freely without me in the room."

She sniffs. "You think so?" I nod. "But what will you do?"

"I have tasks around the house."

"Oh, could you go out and keep an eye on Millie? Please? She gets into the darnedest things."

So I spend much of the day playing with Millie. She calls me Mr. Robot, and I call her Miss Millie, which makes her laugh. She shows me frogs from the creek, and she finds insects and leaves and flowers, and I find their names in online databases. She delights in learning the proper names of things, and everything else that I can share.

Today I was nobody. Mildred slept for most of the day, so I "slept" as well. She woke just now. "I'm hungry" was all she said, but it was enough to wake my empathy net.

Today I am Paul, and Susan, and both Nurse Judys. Mildred's focus drifts. Once I try to be her father, but no one has ever described him to me in detail. I try to synthesize a profile from Henry and Paul; but from the sad look on Mildred's face, I know I failed.

Today I had no name through most of the day, but now I am Paul again. I bring Mildred her dinner, and we have a quiet, peaceful talk about long-gone family pets—long-gone for Paul, but still present for Mildred.

I am just taking Mildred's plate when alerts sound, both audible and in my internal communication net. I check the alerts and find a fire in the basement. I expect the automatic systems to suppress it, but that is not my concern. I must get Mildred to safety.

Mildred looks around the room, panic in her eyes, so I try to project calm. "Come on, Ma. That's the fire drill. You remember fire drills. We have to get you into your chair and outside."

"No!" she shrieks. "I don't like outside."

I check the alerts again. Something has failed in the automatic systems, and the fire is spreading rapidly. Smoke is in Mildred's room already.

I pull the wheelchair up to the bed. "Ma, it's real important we do this drill fast, okay?"

I reach to pull Mildred from the bed, and she screams. "Get away! Who are you? Get out of my house!"

"I'm—" But suddenly I'm nobody. She doesn't recognize me, but I have to try to win her confidence. "I'm Paul, Ma. Now let's move. Quickly!" I pick her up. I'm far too large and strong for her to resist, but I must be careful so she doesn't hurt herself.

The smoke grows thicker. Mildred kicks and screams. Then, when I try to put her into her chair, she stands on her unsteady legs. Before I can stop her, she pushes the chair back with surprising force. It rolls back into the medical monitors, which fall over onto it, tangling it in cables and tubes.

While I'm still analyzing how to untangle the chair, Mildred stumbles toward the bedroom door. The hallway outside has a red glow. Flames lick at the throw rug outside, and I remember the home oxygen tanks in the sitting room down the hall.

I have no time left to analyze. I throw a blanket over Mildred and I scoop her up in my arms. Somewhere deep in my nets is a map of the fire in the house, blocking the halls, but I don't think about it. I wrap the blanket tightly around Mildred, and I crash through the picture window.

We barely escape the house before the fire reaches the tanks. An explosion lifts and tosses us. I was designed as a medical assistant, not an acrobat, and I fear I'll injure Mildred; but though I am not limber, my perceptions are thousands of times faster than human. I cannot twist Mildred out of my way before I hit the ground, so I toss her clear. Then I land, and the impact jars all of my nets for 0.21 seconds.

When my systems stabilize, I have damage alerts all throughout my core, but I ignore them. I feel the heat behind me, blistering my outer cover, and I ignore that as well. Mildred's blanket is burning in multiple places, as is the grass around us. I scramble to my feet, and I roll Mildred on the ground. I'm not indestructible, but I feel no pain and Mildred does, so I do not hesitate to use my hands to pat out the flames.

As soon as the blanket is out, I pick up Mildred, and I run as far from the house as I can get. At the far corner of the garden near the creek, I gently set Mildred down, unwrap her, and feel for her thready pulse.

Mildred coughs and slaps my hands. "Get away from me!" More coughing. "What are you?"

The "what" is too much for me. It shuts down my emulation net, and all I have is the truth. "I am Medical Care Android BRKCX-01932-217JH-98662, Mrs. Owens. I am your caretaker. May I please check that you are well?"

But my empathy net is still online, and I can read terror in every line in Mildred's face. "Metal monster!" she yells. "Metal monster!" She crawls away, hiding under the lilac bush. "Metal!" She falls into an extended coughing spell.

I'm torn between her physical and her emotional health, but physical wins out. I crawl slowly toward her and inject her with a sedative from the medical kit in my chassis. As she slumps, I catch her and lay her carefully on the ground. My empathy net signals a possible shutdown condition, but my concern for her health overrides it. I am programmed for long-term care, not emergency medicine, so I start downloading protocols and integrating them into my storage as I check her for bruises and burns. My kit has salves and painkillers and other supplies to go with my new protocols, and I treat what I can.

But I don't have oxygen, or anything to help with Mildred's coughing. Even sedated, she hasn't stopped. All of my emergency protocols assume I have access to oxygen, so I didn't know what to do.

I am still trying to figure that out when the EMTs arrive and take over Mildred's care. With them on the scene, I am superfluous, and my empathy net finally shuts down.

Today I am Henry. I do not want to be Henry, but Paul tells me that Mildred needs Henry by her side in the hospital. For the end.

Her medical records show that the combination of smoke inhalation, burns, and her already deteriorating condition have proven too much for her. Her body is shutting down faster than medicine can heal it, and the stress has accelerated her mental decline. The doctors have told the family that the kindest thing at this point is to treat her pain, say goodbye, and let her go.

Henry is not talkative at times like this, so I say very little. I sit by Mildred's side and hold her hand as the family comes in for final visits. Mildred drifts in and out. She doesn't know this is goodbye, of course.

Anna is first. Mildred rouses herself enough to smile, and she recognizes her granddaughter. "Anna… child… How is… Ben?" That was Anna's boyfriend almost six years ago. From the look on Anna's face, I can see that she has forgotten Ben already, but Mildred briefly remembers.

"He's… He's fine, Grandma. He wishes he could be here. To say—to see you again." Anna is usually the strong one in the family, but my empathy net says her strength is exhausted. She cannot bear to look at Mildred, so she looks at me; but I am emulating her late grandfather, and that's too much for her as well. She says a few more words, unintelligible even to my auditory inputs. Then she leans over, kisses Mildred, and hurries from the room.

Susan comes in next. Millie is with her, and she smiles at me. I almost emulate Mr. Robot, but my third part keeps me focused until Millie gets bored and leaves. Susan tells trivial stories from her work and from Millie's school. I can't tell if Mildred understands or not, but she smiles and laughs, mostly at appropriate places. I laugh with her.

Susan takes Mildred's hand, and the Henry part of me blinks, surprised. Susan is not openly affectionate under normal circumstances, and especially not toward Mildred. Mother and daughter-in-law have always been cordial, but never close. When I am Paul, I am sure that it is because they are both so much alike. Paul sometimes hums an old song about "just like the one who married dear old dad," but never where either woman can hear him. Now, as Henry, I am touched that Susan has made this gesture but saddened that she took so long.

Susan continues telling stories as we hold Mildred's hands. At some point Paul quietly joins us. He rubs Susan's shoulders and kisses her forehead, and then he steps in to kiss Mildred. She smiles at him, pulls her hand free from mine, and pats his cheek. Then her arm collapses, and I take her hand again.

Paul steps quietly to my side of the bed and rubs my shoulders as well. It comforts him more than me. He needs a father, and an emulation is close enough at this moment.

Susan keeps telling stories. When she lags, Paul adds some of his own, and they trade back and forth. Slowly their stories reach backwards in time, and once or twice Mildred's eyes light as if she remembers those events.

But then her eyes close, and she relaxes. Her breathing quiets and slows, but Susan and Paul try not to notice. Their voices lower, but their stories continue.

Eventually the sensors in my fingers can read no pulse. They have been burned, so maybe they're defective. To be sure, I lean in and listen to Mildred's chest. There is no sound: no breath, no heartbeat.

I remain Henry just long enough to kiss Mildred goodbye. Then I am just me, my empathy net awash in Paul and Susan's grief.

I leave the hospital room, and I find Millie playing in a waiting room and Anna watching her. Anna looks up, eyes red, and I nod. New tears run down her cheeks, and she takes Millie back into Mildred's room.

I sit, and my nets collapse.

Now I am nobody. Almost always.

The cause of the fire was determined to be faulty contract work. There was an insurance settlement. Paul and Susan sold their own home and put both sets of funds into a bigger, better house in Mildred's garden.

I was part of the settlement. The insurance company offered to return me to the manufacturer and pay off my lease, but Paul and Susan decided they wanted to keep me. They went for a full purchase and repair. Paul doesn't understand why, but Susan still fears she may need my services—or Paul might, and I may have to emulate her. She never admits these fears to him, but my empathy net knows.

I sleep most of the time, sitting in my maintenance alcove. I bring back too many memories that they would rather not face, so they leave me powered down for long periods.

But every so often, Millie asks to play with Mr. Robot, and sometimes they decide to indulge her. They power me up, and Miss Millie and I explore all the mysteries of the garden. We built a bridge to the far side of the creek; and on the other side, we're planting daisies. Today she asked me to tell her about her grandmother.

Today I am Mildred.

Martin L. Shoemaker

Martin L. Shoemaker is a programmer who writes on the side...or maybe the other way around. Martin published *UML Applied: A .NET Perspective* with Apress, but a second place win in the Jim Baen Memorial Writing Contest earned him lunch with Buzz Aldrin!

In addition to Writers of the Future vol 31, his work has appeared in *Analog, Clarkesworld, Galaxy's Edge, Digital Science Fiction,* and *Forever Magazine.* His novella, "Murder on the Aldrin Express," was reprinted in *Year's Best Science Fiction Thirty-First Annual Collection* and in *Year's Top Short SF Novels 4*. His short story "Today I Am Paul" was nominated for a Nebula and won the Washington Science Fiction Association Small Press Award before appearing in *Year's Best Science Fiction: Thirty-third Annual Edition* (edited by Gardner Dozois), *The Best Science Fiction of the Year: Volume One* (edited by Neil Clarke), *The Year's Best Science Fiction and Fantasy* (edited by Rich Horton), *Year's Top Ten Tales of Science Fiction 8* (edited by Allen Kaster), and seven international editions (and counting).

More at shoemaker.space.

Today I Am Paul

GotScifi Group

Life's too short. Live more lives. Read.
www.moreLives4me.com

Made in the USA
Columbia, SC
13 June 2018